Then I was in his arms again, and he was kissing me. He kissed my lips, my cheeks and even my hair. It was electrifying. I wanted to stay there forever. If the wind had picked up and carried me out to sea, I wouldn't have cared.

All of a sudden, he lifted his head and looked deep into my eyes. "I don't want this summer ever to end, Lauren," he said.

"Me either," I whispered. I barely got the words out, but it didn't matter. We both knew that something magical was happening.

Dear Readers,

We at Silhouette would like to thank all our readers for your many enthusiastic letters. In direct response to your encouragement, we are now publishing *three* FIRST LOVEs every month.

As always FIRST LOVEs are written especially for and about you—your hopes, your dreams, your ambitions.

Please continue to share your suggestions and comments with us; they play an important part in our pleasing you.

I invite you to write to us at the address below:

> Nancy Jackson
> Senior Editor
> Silhouette Books
> P.O. Box 769
> New York, N.Y. 10019

A SUMMER
TO REMEMBER
Carol Robertson

First Love from Silhouette

Published by Silhouette Books New York

America's Publisher of Contemporary Romance

SILHOUETTE BOOKS, a Simon & Schuster Division of
GULF & WESTERN CORPORATION
1230 Avenue of the Americas, New York, N.Y. 10020

Distributed by Pocket Books

ISBN: 0-671-53352-5

First Silhouette Books printing June, 1983

10 9 8 7 6 5 4 3 2 1

America's Publisher of Contemporary Romance

Printed in the U.S.A.

For Frank

1

We're leaving in exactly one half hour."

That was Dad again. He'd been counting down every half hour for the past two hours. Of course, he had every reason in the world to be worried. Getting the McDermott family out of the house has always been a major production. First of all, Mom triple checks everything from the lock on the back door to the window shades in the upstairs bathroom. And Elizabeth, my little sister, has been absolutely impossible about traveling ever since the time she almost got car sick. But Schnapps, our finicky Schnauzer, is definitely the worst. He hates the car with a passion. It takes three of us and a whole box of People Crackers to lure him inside. Somehow, though, we always manage to get wherever we're going.

"All packed, Lauren?" Dad poked his head into my room and stared with disbelief at the overstuffed suitcase on my bed.

"Just about. I could use some help getting this thing closed."

"I can see that. What on earth is in here?"

"Just the bare essentials. You know, jeans, T-shirts, blouses, shorts, swimsuits, tennis gear, make-up, blow dryer . . ."

"Sorry I asked." Dad laughed.

I had to admit he looked pretty funny sitting on top of my suitcase struggling with the latches.

"There, that should do it," he said, breathing a sigh of relief. "I'll start loading the car."

I had this awful feeling that I'd forgotten something. I took one last look around my room and, sure enough, there it was on my dresser. Randy's locket. That's what I got for taking it off the night before. It's a good thing I saw it in time. I was totally shocked when he gave it to me after Ellen's Valentine's Day party this year. He's usually not the romantic type, but this time he really went all out. It was the most delicate locket I'd ever seen. Real gold and heart-shaped, with flowers engraved on the front. I'd put tiny photos of the two of us inside so I could look at Randy whenever I felt like it.

Well, if I wouldn't be seeing Randy this summer, at least I'd have the locket. Dad came home with the news back in April, but I still hadn't gotten used to the whole idea. He said we'd be spending the entire summer in a beach town called Ocean Bluffs on Fire Island. Mom, Elizabeth, and I would be out there the whole time and Dad would join us for three- or four-day weekends, whatever he could manage.

Some of the other executives at his advertising agency did the same thing, Dad said, and it worked out really well. Fire Island was supposed to be the greatest. It sounded sensational, except for one thing. All my friends were right here in good old Garden City, Long Island. I wouldn't know a soul in Ocean Bluffs.

At least the whole family was together. Last summer had been the absolute pits. Mom and Dad were having some kind of "difficulty communicating," as Mom used to say, so Dad moved to an apartment in New York City. Mom said they just needed to be apart for a while to work things out. Dad said he was under a lot of pressure at the agency. I thought it was a pretty dirty trick. I mean, one minute everything's rolling along just fine and the next thing you know—right out of the blue—your parents are separated and you feel like some kind of freak.

"Ellen's on the phone, Lauren," Mom called from down the hall. "Don't stay on too long. We're just about ready," she whispered, handing me the receiver.

"Hi, El. What are you doing up so early?"

"I just wanted to say good-bye one more time. And guess what? My parents finally said I could come out to visit you for a few days in July!"

"Fantastic! But I still wish you were going to be there for the whole summer."

"Listen, have a great time and don't forget to keep in touch."

"Don't worry. I'll write and give you all the details. I'll see you in July, El."

"Adios."

I felt a little sad when I went back into my room. I couldn't imagine not talking to Ellen three times a day. I stared into the mirror over my dresser and began to brush my hair. I guess my long, dark hair is my best feature. It's certainly better than my eyes, which are a nice shade of blue, but much too close together, or my nose, which is far too big. I glanced down at the picture of Randy that was taped to the mirror. What could be keeping him? Last night he told me that he'd stop over on the way to work, and it wasn't like him to be late. If I didn't see him before I left, I'd be miserable.

I could tell by the way Schnapps was shrieking that it was almost time to go. I ran downstairs, and right on schedule Mom was making the final security check and Elizabeth was whimpering about how she'd rather sit in the front seat next to the window.

"In case you're interested, Randy's outside," Elizabeth whined, breezing right by me.

I met him on the front steps just as he was about to ring the doorbell. His shiny dark hair was getting a little long, just the way I liked it, and his deep brown eyes were sparkling.

"Looks like you're all set to go," he said. He seemed to be hiding something behind his back.

"Yeah, believe it or not I think we're finally going to get this show on the road."

"Here, this is for you." He was holding a perfect red rose.

"Randy, it's gorgeous! Thank you." I held it up to my nose and gave it a good, long sniff.

"I'm really going to miss you, Laur. You'll probably break every guy's heart on Fire Island."

"Oh, sure. And what about you?" I teased. "Now

that you're a big hero lifeguard, the girls at the pool will be hanging around you in swarms."

Before I could say another thing, he put his arms around my waist and kissed me softly. I took a deep breath and tried not to cry. Saying good-bye was bad enough without a bunch of tears all over the place.

"You know, Randy, it's going to be pretty lonely without you. You have my address, right?"

"Right. I'm not much at writing letters, but I'll give it a shot."

From the commotion inside, it sounded like everyone was on their way out.

"Well, Laur, I guess this is it. Have a great summer."

"I'll try."

He kissed me again quickly and walked across the front lawn to his old red Volkswagen. He looked completely adorable in his baggy lifeguard T-shirt and his faded blue denim cutoffs.

"Hey, Randy," I called as he was getting into his Beetle. "Thanks again for the rose."

He turned and waved and then drove off, honking the horn twice, just like he always did.

I didn't even have a chance to get upset or anything. I was whisked into the car and we were off. If there's one thing that drives me crazy, it's sitting next to Elizabeth in the back seat. Good old Elizabeth is one of a kind. I call her the midget fidget. She usually starts by asking me if she can look through the pictures in my wallet and I have to explain for the hundredth time who everyone is. Then she has to have a Life Saver or a piece of gum or something, which I gladly give her if she promises to be quiet for at least fifteen minutes. She invariably has to go to the bathroom when there isn't a gas station around for miles. And Schnapps only makes things worse by constantly running back and forth from window to window, barking his head off at the passing cars.

"How many more minutes till we get there?" Elizabeth was already squirming around.

"We just pulled out of the driveway," I groaned.

I wondered if I'd survive the ride. I picked up Randy's rose and ran my fingers across the soft petals. I'd been going out with him for over a year now, but sometimes I just didn't understand him. One minute he'd want to arm wrestle, "just for fun," and the next minute he'd be bringing me flowers. Men. I decided I wouldn't even try to figure him out.

"How come Randy gave you a rose?" Elizabeth chirped.

"It's sort of a going-away present," I said, carefully tucking it into my canvas bag.

"Are you guys in love or something?"

"Elizabeth! What kind of a question is that?"

"Well, the two of you act weird sometimes."

"Tell you what, Elizabeth. I'll give you a piece of gum if you can find a license plate from Alaska, okay?"

That should've kept her occupied.

I'd always thought that love was for older girls, not for seventeen-year-olds. Especially this seventeen-year-old. But sometimes I wondered about the way I felt about Randy. He was like a super best friend. You know, someone to talk to. Someone who was always there. But don't get me wrong. He was my boyfriend too.

I'll never forget the first time I saw him. It's funny.

We'd both been going to Garden City High for a couple of years, but it wasn't until last fall that I really noticed him. "Noticed" is putting it mildly. He practically knocked my socks off. Ellen and I decided to go to a swim meet after school. I don't know what it was, but as soon as they introduced him— "Randy Bryant, co-captain of the Garden City High School swim team"—I knew I had to go out with him. He looked so confident as he stood there by the edge of the pool, waiting for the meet to begin. Ellen and I agreed that out of all the guys on the team, he had the nicest build and the cutest smile. Maybe that was it. And the way he shook his head when he came out of the water to get the wet hair out of his eyes. That too. He really got to me. Ellen said she thought he had been in her sixth-grade class, but she couldn't really remember much about him. Of course, I bugged her until she introduced me.

Two weeks later Ellen and I just happened to run into him after swim practice. He didn't ask me out that day, but at least he finally knew who I was. Then, the following week, when I saw him at the Fireplace, he asked me to go to a movie. We were going to double with Ellen and Tom. I nearly died. We'd been going strong ever since. We weren't officially going steady, you see, but we sort of had an understanding.

I guess you never really know for sure, though. I mean, look at Mom and Dad. They were married twenty years and then all of a sudden something went wrong. Sure, everything worked out okay, but I learned one thing. You never know what's around the bend when it comes to love. Mom says love is a full-time job and you have to work at it every minute. I'd never admit this to anyone except maybe Ellen, but sometimes I wonder if it's really worth all that work.

I wish I could be as matter-of-fact about love as Ellen. She's always saying that you'll definitely know it when it hits you. I'm crazy about Randy, but I'm not sure I'm actually in love with him or anything. So I guess this isn't the real thing. Or is it?

2

I decided to spend my first new morning on Fire Island at the beach. Our house, "A Summer Place," was just a stone's throw from the ocean, so I could practically fall out of bed and be there. I thought I'd scope out the rest of the island later.

I grabbed a towel and some suntan lotion and walked to the end of my block and then down the wooden steps that led from the dunes to the beach. The hot morning sun felt fantastic. I spread out my towel on the sand and covered myself with lotion. All I could hear was the sound of waves breaking on the shore. It couldn't have been more peaceful.

I was almost asleep when a Frisbee landed about two inches from my nose, spraying sand all over my face.

"Sorry," a male voice mumbled.

"Hey, would you watch what you're doing!" I

growled in my nastiest tone, which I usually reserved for Elizabeth. *Then* I opened my eyes. I caught a glimpse of him as he picked up the Frisbee and ran off. Leave it to me to open my mouth and in two seconds flat scare off the most gorgeous guy I've ever seen. Sandy blond hair. Very tan. Didn't catch the color of his eyes. Broad shoulders. Long legs. If Ellen were here she'd say "definitely a hunk."

He was playing Frisbee with his dog, a beautiful Irish setter. As he tossed the Frisbee, the dog would run along the beach, jump up, and then catch it in his mouth. Well, most of the time, anyway. Sometimes it landed in the water and the dog would have to do some pretty fancy swimming to retrieve it. I almost wished it would land on my towel again. Before long they had run all the way down the beach and were completely out of view. I felt a little guilty for a minute, but then I figured there was nothing wrong with just looking at another guy. I'd probably never see him again, anyway. And after the way I snapped at him, he probably thought I was the biggest grouch in the world.

I closed my eyes and wondered about Randy back home. I could just picture him at the pool, sitting on the lifeguard stand, looking great in his red lifeguard trunks and his floppy old visor. I promised myself I'd write to him sometime today. Before I left we had both agreed that it would be okay to go on a couple of casual dates with other people if we really wanted to. I'd never thought of myself as the jealous type, but I just couldn't stand the thought of someone else being with Randy. You know, riding next to him in his Volkswagen and doing all the special things we did. Maybe I shouldn't have been so possessive, but he was my boyfriend, steady or not. If he went out with anyone else while I was away, I didn't want to know.

As for me, I decided to play it by ear. I certainly didn't want another boyfriend. One was about all I could handle.

I must have been lying in the sun for at least a couple of hours. I couldn't figure out if it was the heat or what, but my thoughts kept drifting back to that adorable guy with the Frisbee. I wondered if he could be staying here on Fire Island for the whole summer. Or maybe he was just visiting for the day. Oh well, what was the difference? I had my big chance and I blew it. A hunk like him would never even notice me, anyway. Every once in a while I looked around but there was no sign of him. How could I be so curious about him and miss Randy like crazy at the same time? It didn't make sense.

I decided it was time to check out the scenery. Besides, I was getting positively deep-fried lying so still. I got up and walked down to the water, but as soon as I put one toe in I ruled out the possibility of going for a swim. It was ice cold. I strolled up the beach, picking up sea shells and pieces of driftwood along the way. Then, all of a sudden, I stumbled upon the most incredible sand castle I'd ever seen. It was at least four feet wide, with three different levels, a courtyard inside and several turrets. There was even a moat around it. It was a lot more creative than anything I had ever made. A girl about my age was working on it.

"That's pretty amazing," I commented.

"Thanks. I've been working all morning. Some crazy dog plowed right through it before."

She had a funny accent, but I couldn't quite place it. It wasn't foreign or anything, just different.

"Did he have a Frisbee?" I asked.

"What?"

"Never mind," I mumbled, chuckling to myself about the spirited Irish setter. "Are you here for the summer?" I watched her carefully patch a leak in the moat.

"Yes. I'm with my mother. We're staying here in Ocean Bluffs." She didn't take her eyes off her work for a minute. "How about you?"

"We're staying in Ocean Bluffs, too. On Sandy Lane. We just got here yesterday."

"I've been here a couple of weeks already. It's a terrific island. Would you mind handing me that pail of water over there?"

"Here you are. Is there anything I can do to help?" I didn't know the first thing about sand castles, but I thought I'd offer, anyway.

"Thanks, but I'm just about finished." She added one more handful of sand to the largest turret. "There, that should do it. What do you think? Is it medieval enough?"

We both stepped back and admired her work.

"I think it's great and it's definitely medieval. I can almost see the knights jousting in the court-yard."

"Me too!" She laughed. "By the way, my name is Kimberly Preston."

"Mine's Lauren McDermott."

It's funny the way you can meet someone and know right off that you're going to be friends. That's the feeling I had about Kimberly. She was so natural and easy to talk to. I was glad I'd found her.

"Where are you from, Kimberly?"

"Please call me Kim. I'm from Boston, but this fall Mother and I will be moving to Port Washington on Long Island."

"I don't live very far from there. I'm from Garden City."

"I'm going to miss Boston, but Mother got transferred and there was nothing we could do." Her voice sort of faded out and she looked a little sad, but before I could say anything she quickly changed the subject. "Listen," she went on, "since you just got here, would you like me to show you around a little? We could go into Ocean Beach. That's the big city out here."

"Sounds perfect."

We walked along the water for about a mile and a half until we got to Ocean Beach. It was a quaint little village and the only place on the island where you could really shop. It had a big open plaza—well, big for Fire Island, anyway—with lots of stores and restaurants around it. But just like the rest of the island, there were no cars and no real roads. Just a few Jeeps and dune buggies here and there.

"Do you think Stuart's General Store carries tennis balls, Kim? I desperately need some new ones."

"Probably. Let's go in and take a look."

"Do you play?" I asked, hoping I'd found a partner.

"Are you kidding? When it comes to sports, I'm a klutz on wheels."

"Well, we're even. When it comes to sand castles, *I'm* the klutz!"

Stuart's General Store seemed to have a little bit

19

of everything. We made our way to the back, where most of the sports equipment was displayed. Everything on the shelves was packed so tightly that it was practically impossible to find anything. We just wandered around for a while.

Suddenly I stopped dead in my tracks. There he was at the end of the aisle. The guy with the Frisbee. No question. Same blond hair, same broad shoulders. I couldn't believe it. He was walking toward us. My heart started doing about ninety miles an hour.

"I think the tennis balls are in the next aisle," Kim said.

I heard her voice but it didn't really sink in.

"Lauren?"

I just stared at her blankly.

"Are you there, Lauren?"

"What?" I muttered.

"Are you okay?" she asked, sounding concerned.

"He's coming over here," I whispered.

"Who?"

"The guy with the Frisbee."

"What? What guy? What Frisbee?"

"What am I going to do?" Panic was setting in fast.

"Hello, may I help you?" he interrupted.

Oh, he works here, I thought. Why weren't any words coming out of my mouth? All I could do was stare, and I prayed he wouldn't recognize me. Those few seconds of silence seemed like an eternity.

"She'd like some tennis balls, please," Kim chimed in, nudging my side with her elbow.

"Step right this way," he said, pointing straight ahead.

We followed him to the next aisle. I was pretty surprised that my feet remembered how to walk.

"I'd recommend Spalding," he explained, stepping in front of a large display. "I find the green balls are easier to see in the bright sun around here, but it's up to you."

My face was burning. It must have been beet red. I didn't know if my mouth would be working but I decided to give it a try. "Fine, I'll take two cans of the green. Do I pay you?"

"Me? Why would you pay me? I don't actually work here. I just wanted to meet you." He paused for a second and smiled. "Didn't I see you on the beach this morning?"

I'd been set up! I thought I was going to fall over and die right then and there. Could this be happening to *me*?

He was grinning from ear to ear, looking just as cool as he could be.

"So you play tennis, huh?" he went on.

"Uh, yeah, just a little," I choked.

"How about a few games tomorrow morning?"

"I don't know. I'm not very good." Why did I say that? I always manage to blurt out the wrong thing.

"Hey, don't worry about it. I'll meet you at the Ocean Bluffs courts tomorrow at eleven, okay?"

"Okay." I did it.

He vanished before I realized that I hadn't even gotten his name. I guess I'll find out tomorrow.

Kim had been looking on with amazement the whole time.

"What was that all about?"

After I came back down to planet earth I told her all about the Frisbee, the Irish setter, and Randy.

We went across the plaza to Barnacle Bill's for Cokes and tuna salad sandwiches. She agreed that The Guy with the Frisbee, as we called him, was a first-class hunk. We figured he was a little older. Probably in college.

"What do you suppose his name is?" I wondered. I pushed my sandwich aside. I couldn't even think about eating.

"I don't know. He looks kind of like a Jeff or a Ken."

"What if he's a fabulous tennis player? I won't even be able to return his serve. I just know it."

"Then he'll help your game. Will you stop worrying?"

Stop worrying, I thought. That's a laugh.

Ten fifty the next day. Just about time to leave. I didn't want to get there too early and seem overanxious. Keep them waiting, that's what Ellen always says. He probably booked court time, though, so I didn't want to be too late, either. If I walked slowly, I'd be there right on time. I grabbed my racket and my can of new tennis balls and I was on my way.

As I approached the courts I could see that he was already there. He had his back to me as he smashed one serve after another over the net. I was terrified. This was going to be even worse than I thought.

Sooner or later I had to let him know I was there, but I couldn't get up enough nerve to talk to him. My stomach was still in one big knot. I just stood there for a couple of minutes trying to get my act together. "Hi," I finally called. Real original.

"Oh, hi." He turned around and flashed his gorgeous smile. He was wearing white tennis shorts and a pale blue Kings Point Prep T-shirt that was exactly the color of his eyes. I had trouble keeping both feet on the ground. I was falling head over heels and I didn't even know his name. "I was just getting in a little practice," he went on.

"Looks pretty good. You know, I don't think I caught your name yesterday."

"Oh, yeah. Sorry. I'm Brad Caldwell."

"Lauren McDermott."

"Nice to meet you, Lauren McDermott. Want to hit a few around?"

"Sure."

"I'll send one over to your baseline, okay?" he said, bouncing a ball at his side.

"Okay." Here goes nothing, I thought.

My whole arm stung from the impact as I tried to return the ball. It didn't quite make it back over the net. In fact, it didn't even travel five feet. It just sort of fizzled out. I was pretty embarrassed.

"Let's try one one," he yelled. "Step back a little."

I took his advice and moved back behind the baseline. This time I sent the ball over the net without too much difficulty. I began to feel a little more confident. If we kept on like this, I might do okay. We volleyed back and forth for a few minutes until we used up all the balls.

"I thought you said you weren't any good," he shouted as he picked up some stray balls by the net.

"I'm not."

"Are you kidding? You have a wicked backhand."

"Thanks. You're not so bad yourself."

"How about a game or two?"

"Forget it. You'll destroy me."

"That modesty routine didn't work the first time, remember? I have this strange feeling that you'll give me a run for my money. What've you got to lose?"

"Just a couple of games." I laughed.

"I'll even let you serve first."

"Oh, all right. You're on."

Well, that was lucky. Serving first was my only hope for staying in the game. It's not that my serve is impossible to hit. Far from it. In fact, it has all the power of a lead meatball. It's just that I always manage to put it in the right place.

I have to admit I made some pretty dumb mistakes. Like the time I lobbed the ball right over the fence and out of the court, and the time I ran furiously for the big smash—smack into the net. Brad beat me hands down, but at least he didn't totally laugh me off the courts. I scored a few pretty good points and I may have taken him by surprise a couple of times.

"I'm impressed, but I'm not surprised," he said, running toward the net.

"What do you mean?"

"I could tell by your legs that you'd play a good game."

"Oh, really?" My cheeks were turning pink.

"Yeah, really. Long stride. Very athletic."

I don't think anyone ever noticed my legs before.

"Where'd you learn to play?" he asked.

"At school. I'd like to try out for the team next year. Last year I was cut in the final round of tryouts."

"Tough break. I'd say you have a pretty decent shot this year if you keep it up. I don't know about you but I'm parched. Want to go over to Sprinkles? They have the best lemonade on the island."

My heart started to pound. "Okay." I tried to sound as nonchalant as possible, but I was ready to go into orbit.

We sat under a green-and-white-striped umbrella looking at the colorful sailboats in the bay. They were so pretty against the deep blue water and the pale sky. They almost looked like toys.

"I've never seen you around Fire Island before, Lauren. Is this your first summer?"

"As a matter of fact it is."

"What do you think?"

"Well, it's only been a few days, but I absolutely love it so far. Do you live in Ocean Bluffs?"

"No, my family has a place in Sea Gate, the next town up the beach."

Wow. Kim had told me about Sea Gate. It's an old, wealthy community. You couldn't even get in unless you lived there or were someone's guest. It had its own private ferry and a beach club. Brad didn't seem to be making a big deal about living there, though.

"Do you come here every summer?" I asked.

"Ever since I was a little kid. It just wouldn't be summer without Fire Island."

We sat and talked for a while, enjoying the cool breeze from the bay. He told me his home was in Kings Point on Long Island and that he was entering Princeton in the fall. Small wonder he was such a fantastic tennis player. He played on the varsity team in prep school and he was just about assured a spot on the Princeton team next year. Ditto for soccer.

"Listen, Lauren, I have a great idea. Sea Gate has a tennis tournament every year. How'd you like to be my partner in the mixed doubles competition?"

"Oh, Brad, I don't think I'm good enough for a tournament."

"Will you cut that stuff out! You play a terrific game. Besides, I think we'd make a great pair, don't you?"

"I don't know. I'll need lots of practice."

"I'll coach you. Come on, it'll be fun."

He was flashing that smile again. I couldn't resist.

"Well, the practice would help me make the team next year. Okay, it's a deal."

"Fantastic. Listen, I've got to be getting home," he said as he picked up the rackets. "An old friend of mine is coming in on the two o'clock ferry and I promised I'd meet him. Can I walk you back?"

When we got to my door, he looked right at me with those incredible blue eyes. I thought I would melt.

"Same time, same place, tomorrow?"

"You mean tennis again?" I asked.

"You bet. If we're going to be in the tournament, we're really going to have to practice."

"Fine with me. And Brad, thanks for the game today."

"Anytime. See you tomorrow."

He ran off before I could blink an eye. I was ready to burst when I ran into the house to call Kim. We decided to meet down at the beach for the afternoon. I took a quick shower and changed into my turquoise strapless bathing suit.

I got down to the beach before Kim. I hate being

first and having to wait all alone. What was taking her so long? I was dying to tell her the whole story about that morning. I tried reading a magazine to pass the time but it was no use. I just couldn't concentrate on anything.

I finally saw her running barefoot across the red-hot sand. She was probably burning her feet off.

"Should have worn my sandals," she complained as she darted straight onto my towel. She spread out her stuff next to mine and I told her all about my morning and about the tournament in Sea Gate. She could see that I was excited.

"This sounds pretty serious," she said.

"Kim, I've never known anyone like him in my whole life."

"What about Randy?"

"Don't get me wrong, Kim, Randy's really great. But Brad's different. He's so sophisticated. He's older and he's going to college. You know what I mean."

"Yeah, that's terrific, but don't forget we just met him yesterday."

"What's the matter? Don't you like him?"

"Sure I like him. I just think we should find out a little bit more about him, that's all."

I knew she was right but I wasn't in the mood to listen to the voice of reason. I couldn't help the way I felt about Brad. Just thinking about him was exciting. But I did wonder whether or not he had a girlfriend back home—or even here in Sea Gate, for that matter. Oh, who cares, I thought, I'm having fun and it's summer vacation, and that's all that matters.

"Let's go for a swim before I absolutely burn up." If I sat there thinking about Brad all afternoon, I knew I'd drive myself crazy.

"Lydia and I were thinking of going to a movie tonight," Kim said. "Want to come along?"

"No thanks. I think I'll write some letters and turn in early. Who's Lydia? A new kid?"

Kim laughed. "No, my mother. I've been calling her by her first name ever since the divorce."

"Your parents are divorced?"

"Oh, I thought I'd told you. It's been nearly two years now. Sometimes it's a hassle, but I try to make the best of it."

"Wow. It must be really tough."

I wanted to ask her a million questions, but I didn't want to sound nosy or anything. Divorce had been my big fear ever since Mom and Dad's separation. I knew everything was supposed to be okay between them, but still, I couldn't be totally sure. Sometimes it seemed that there was this big cloud in the distance just waiting to burst.

"The hardest part," Kim went on, "is that you have to split up your life. We can't share things together like we used to."

"Does your father live up in Boston?"

"Yeah. Dad's an English professor at Boston University. He'll be in London on sabbatical for the rest of the summer, but then I'm supposed to visit him in Boston every other weekend starting this fall."

"That'll be nice."

"I guess. I really love seeing him and Boston is the greatest—especially the university—but it'll be hard to meet new kids when we move to Long Island if I'm in Boston all the time. That's what I mean about feeling split in half. I'd rather have Dad here."

"Don't worry. I'll introduce you to everyone at home," I said, feeling sympathetic.

"Thanks, Lauren. Hey, listen," she added, studying the worried look on my face, "it's really not all that bad. Lydia and I have a great time together, and whenever I see Dad he's really terrific. Sometimes I just get a little sad because things aren't the way they used to be."

"Sure. I understand." I wanted to say something about Mom and Dad, but I just couldn't get up enough courage to talk about it. Maybe some other time. I had other things on my mind, anyway. Like Brad.

I was in a daze for the rest of the day. I don't think I said ten words at dinner. Mom kept asking me what was wrong while I was helping her with the dishes, but I just said I was tired from tennis. You know how it is. I didn't want to go into the whole thing about Brad. I knew it would get too intense. I just wanted to retreat to my room so I could write to Randy and get a good night's sleep for tennis the next day.

As soon as I got upstairs I took some stationery out of my night table drawer and propped up my pillow behind my back. Schnapps jumped on the bed and curled up at my feet. Hopefully Elizabeth wouldn't burst in and start asking a million questions.

Dear Randy,
    Sorry it's taken so long to write.

Wonderful. So now what am I going to say? I'm sure not going to tell him about Brad and the tournament. Not in a letter, anyway. And maybe not ever. Besides, there wasn't even anything to tell. Yet. I stared at the ceiling for a while and then went on.

You wouldn't believe how beautiful Fire Island is. I've met some terrific kids. One girl came all the way from Boston.

I've been playing tennis and swimming in the ocean like crazy. Next week Dad's taking us all sailing in the bay. I want to try some clamming too.

How are things at work? I hope you'll be able to get some time off so you can come for a visit. You'd just love it here.

Love,
Laur

Randy was the only person who called me Laur all the time. I kind of liked it. I wondered if he'd really visit. I sure would have my hands full if he did.

P.S. I miss you.

3

After tennis practice Brad invited Kim and me to the beach at Sea Gate. Everything I'd heard about Sea Gate was true. It was beautiful. The old Victorian Sea Gate Beach Club was perched high above us in the dunes. From the beach you could see its big patio and bright yellow umbrellas. There were lots of old Victorian homes set around it. I wondered which one was Brad's.

The three of us were lying near the water, reading and soaking up the sun. Every muscle ached from our morning tennis match. The hot sun was just what I needed. It felt almost like a massage.

Every time I stole a glance at Brad stretched out on his towel, my heart started to beat a little faster. How was I supposed to resist him? Nobody could.

"Brad Caldwell! What a surprise!"

A pretty blonde was standing over him.

"Oh, hi," Brad said, barely looking up from his science fiction novel. "Jenny, I'd like you to meet Lauren and Kim," he added, as if suddenly remembering his manners.

"Nice to meet you," Jenny said distantly, never taking her eyes off Brad.

"Same here," I managed.

"Are you girls new in Sea Gate?"

"No, we're from Ocean Bluffs," Kim replied.

"Oh, yes, of course," Jenny said, as if that explained everything.

"Will I see you at the club tonight?" she asked, turning to Brad.

"Could be," he said noncommittally.

"Well, I'll certainly be there. Mother's on the social committee, you know. As a matter of fact, I was just on my way up there to help with some of the arrangements. I really must run. I hope to see you tonight, Brad."

We all watched her slowly turn and practically float up the beach. Of course, she looked perfect in her tiny bikini. Not an ounce of fat on her.

"Anybody feel like going for a walk?" Brad asked.

"You guys go ahead." Kim yawned. "I'm too comfortable to move."

Brad and I started walking along the water toward Bay Park, the next town beyond Sea Gate. I wished he would take my hand, but I guess it was just as well that he didn't. My palms were kind of sweaty and gross from all the greasy suntan lotion and sand.

"I think we made some real progress on the courts today. We've got a great chance at the mixed doubles title, don't you think, Lauren?"

"Yeah, I guess so," I said flatly. I was preoccupied with Jenny.

"You don't sound very enthusiastic. Where's the old team spirit?"

"Oh, sorry. My mind was wandering a little."

"Listen, I forgot to mention this yesterday. I was so psyched about tennis. There's a big barbecue at the club tonight. Do you want to go?"

So that's what she was babbling about. The social committee and all that nonsense.

"I'd love to, Brad. The only thing is I have plans with Kim." Wouldn't you just know it.

"I may have a solution but I didn't want to say anything in front of her."

"Well?"

"I have this friend from school named Mike who just came out here. Remember, I had to meet his ferry yesterday?"

"Yeah, so?"

"I think Kim would really like him. What if we set them up on a blind date for tonight?"

"Brad, that's a great idea."

"Good, 'cause I already dropped a subtle hint to Mike and he's all for it."

I felt like hugging him.

We went back to the blankets, and after considerable coaxing Kim finally agreed to go out with Mike. But when we left Brad and walked back to Ocean Bluffs, she seemed to be having second thoughts.

"How do I know he's not a complete nerd?"

"If he's a friend of Brad's how bad could he be?" I asked.

"True. So what should I wear to this thing, anyway?"

"I'm sure jeans and a nice top will be fine. That's what I'm wearing. It's only a barbecue."

We reached the point where I turned off to go down Sandy Lane.

"I'll see you tonight, Kim. And don't worry. It'll be a lot of fun."

"Hey, Kim," I called after I was halfway down my block. "If Mike turns out to be a total nerd I'll rescue you, I promise."

"Thanks a bunch," she yelled back. "I'll be over later."

Mom was in the kitchen making a salad when I got home. Everyone says I look just like her. Sometimes I see the resemblance. I'm five feet six, two inches taller than she is, but we have the same smile and the same blue eyes and dark brown hair. I don't think I'm as pretty as she is, though.

Naturally I could hardly wait to tell her my big news. I knew she'd be pleased to hear I was making friends. She was kind of worried—what with Dad and everything—that we kids wouldn't have such a great summer.

"Hey, Mom, guess what? Brad invited me to a barbecue tonight at the Sea Gate Beach Club."

I poured myself a glass of iced tea.

"That's lovely, dear. You're seeing a lot of him, aren't you?"

"Yeah, I guess so, between tennis and all. You'll get to meet him tonight. He's coming over with his friend Mike to pick up Kim and me. Any mail?" I added.

"Yes. There's a letter for you on the table."

I sprinted across the room, grabbed the letter, and immediately turned it over to look at the return address. Randy. I couldn't believe it. He must have written the moment I left. I ran up to my room and tore it open.

Dear Laur,
    Just wanted to tell you that I miss you already. It's going to be pretty boring around here without you. I guess the pool will keep me busy, and I'm finally going to help Dad repave the driveway. That's all for now. Not a whole lot to say, since I just saw you.
    Be good and write soon. Ellen says hi.
                                                    Love,
                                                    Randy

I felt pretty rotten about having a date already. But then again, my date with Brad wasn't a real date. It was only a double date and that didn't really count. In any event, I knew that if I didn't get into the shower soon I'd never be ready on time. I got my stuff together and then went out to the deck.

The best thing about A Summer Place was the outdoor shower. It was made out of natural-colored wood, and when it got all steamed up it felt just like a sauna. It had a skylight in the ceiling, so when you looked up you really felt like you were out in the open. I just stood there under the hot water thinking about Brad and Randy. No question about it: I had a serious case of the guilties. Well, there was nothing I could do about it now. I'd made the date with Brad and that was that. The weird thing was that even though I felt bad, I still wanted to go.

After I dried off and wrapped myself in my cuddly white terry cloth robe, I went back up to my room. I couldn't help thinking about that afternoon as I carefully maneuvered the blow dryer.

"Will I see you at the club tonight, Brad? Mother's on the committee," I mimicked, batting my eyelashes into the mirror.

Jenny was definitely going to be a problem.

When my hair was dry, I pinned it up on top of my head until it was time to go. I don't know why I bothered. It would only frizz up once it hit the sea air. Then I took out my favorite white camisole, the one with the pretty flowers embroidered on the front. It had a matching white jacket that I could bring along in case it got chilly later.

I looked at myself carefully in the mirror and decided I didn't need too much makeup. My face was starting to get pretty tan. A little mascara, blusher, and some wine-tinted lip gloss did it.

I was almost ready when I heard Elizabeth running down the hall.

"Kim's here," she said, as she came in and bounced on the bed next to Schnapps.

"Would you do me a huge favor? Tell her I'll be down in a minute."

"Okay. See ya." She flew out of the room.

I brushed my hair one more time and added a tiny bit more gloss to my lips. I was almost out the door when I remembered perfume. I sprayed some on each wrist and went downstairs.

The doorbell rang just as I got down to the living room. Schnapps leaped at the door and started jumping up and down. His standard greeting. Kim looked very relieved. Mike was definitely not a nerd. And I could tell that my parents were impressed with Brad. He could really pour on the charm.

It was such a gorgeous night that we decided to take the long route up to Sea Gate. The sun was setting over the bay in deep shades of red and burned orange. By the time we got to the club, it was almost dark. The outdoor patio and the beach below it were lit up with colorful lanterns.

Fortunately Kim and Mike seemed to be getting along pretty well. The four of us hadn't stopped talking and laughing since we left the house.

We were sitting on the patio eating hamburgers and minding our own business when Her Royal Blondeness descended upon us. I knew it was inevitable.

"Having a good time, Brad?" Jenny sang, ignoring everyone else. She looked perfect, natch, in a beautiful cotton print sundress.

"The best, Jenny. It's a great party."

"Good. Mother will be pleased. Her committee worked so hard. You know, Brad, I haven't seen you around the tennis courts this year."

"I guess you haven't been looking hard enough, Jenny."

"Well, I've already started practicing for the tournament. Scott Harrington and I plan to take the mixed doubles title in one clean sweep."

"I wouldn't be too sure about that if I were you," Brad said smoothly.

"Who could possibly beat us?"

"Yeah, I guess you're right." He shot a knowing glance my way. We'd show her a thing or two.

"If you'll excuse me, Brad, there's Scott now. See you around. Nice to see you again, Laura."

Kim rolled her eyes as soon as Jenny disappeared. I had no idea what kind of a tennis player old Jenny was, but I made up my mind that Brad and I were going to beat her if it killed us.

"Look at that old rickety house in the dunes," Kim said.

"Where?" I asked, looking up.

"To the left. The one with the windows boarded up."

"That's Captain McGuire's place," Brad said. "He was an old sea captain whose ship was lost about fifty years ago. Everyone assumes he's dead but no one's really sure. The house has been abandoned. It's supposed to be haunted."

"Oh, come on." I laughed.

"It's true. The front door opens and slams all the time and sometimes you see smoke coming out of the chimney, but there's never anyone there. Every once and a while someone claims to have seen the old man. He smokes a pipe and has a long gray beard. Oh yeah, and he wears his captain's hat too."

"Brad, you're joking," Kim said.

"I couldn't be more serious."

"Well, have you ever gone inside the house?"

"Me? Are you kidding? When it comes to stuff like that, I'm your basic chicken."

"Brad, the house couldn't really be haunted," I said.

"I wouldn't want to find out. Believe me, it's pretty scary looking. Someday I'll take you over there and you'll see what I mean."

The conversation turned from ghosts to science fiction movies and Kim and Mike were soon engrossed in a discussion about the special effects in *Star Wars*.

"I'm just not into this," Brad said, taking me aside. "Let's go for a walk."

We took off our shoes, rolled up our jeans, and walked down the old stone steps to the beach. It was pitch black except for the moonlight. I didn't know if it was the cool sea breeze or Brad, but I had tiny goosebumps all over my arms.

"Oh, darn, I left my jacket up on the patio."

"Don't worry about it. I'll keep you warm," he said as he put his arm around my waist. When we got to the water, we just stood there for a while staring out into the darkness.

"So tell me about yourself, Lauren."

"I don't know where to start."

"Start at the beginning."

"Well, I'm really pretty ordinary. I was born in Garden City General Hospital and I've lived in Garden City all my life. I have a little sister. I love tennis, I play the piano, and I want to be a physical therapist. How about you?" I added, before he could ask any questions. I didn't want to tell Brad the unordinary stuff. You know, about my parents' problems. He might think I was weird or something.

"I was born in Chicago and we moved to Kings Point when I was seven. I have an older brother who's a lawyer and a younger brother who's a pain. I'm majoring in pre-law at Princeton. How do you like me so far?"

"Great. Tell me more."

"I can't give away all my secrets so soon." He looked deep into my eyes and smiled.

The next thing I knew he was holding me in his arms.

"You know, Lauren, I'm glad I found you. You're not stuck-up or anything, like a lot of girls I know."

I didn't know what to say but it didn't really matter. He held me closer and kissed me. I wanted that moment to last forever. I felt kind of light-headed, like everything around me was spinning. He kissed me again and I practically melted right into his arms. I finally rested my head on his shoulder.

"Let's walk up the beach," he whispered, gently stroking my hair.

I started to shiver, but I knew it wasn't from the cold.

"Brad, I really think we should be getting back. It's freezing out here." I hoped he bought my excuse.

"Hey, you're shivering. Here, take this." He pulled off his big fisherman's sweater and draped it around my shoulders as we headed across the beach and back to the club.

4

I opened my eyes and squinted to read the alarm clock on my night table. Ten thirty. I hate sleeping late. It makes me feel groggy all day. I glanced across the room and saw that Elizabeth's bed was already made. I'm amazed that I didn't hear her get up. She's about as quiet as a demolition crew in the morning. I must have been out like a light.

I kicked off the covers but I was too lazy to get up just yet. I just lay there thinking. I hoped Brad didn't think I was weird or anything for not having wanted to walk up the beach with him. I don't know what happened to me. I sort of panicked after he kissed me. Well, maybe next time I wouldn't be so jumpy.

I finally sat up and looked out the window over my bed. It was a fantastic beach day. No wonder the house was so quiet. I put on my robe and padded downstairs to the kitchen to make some breakfast.

Nothing elaborate, just some O.J. and a cup of tea. I wandered around the kitchen for a minute and then headed for the living room. As I curled up on the sofa, I noticed the new July issue of *Harper's* on the coffee table. Mom read it from cover to cover every month, but I was only interested in one thing. I quickly opened to the horoscopes on the last page and ran my index finger down the columns until I found my sign.

ARIES

THE RAM/MARCH 21–APRIL 20

July will find you happy but confused. Venus has brought a new romance into your life but it may become complicated after the 7th. Trust your own instincts.

Hmmm. Between Randy and Brad, how much more complicated could it get? I read on.

Your Aries energy will abound mid-month and you'll have ample opportunity to take part in outdoor activities. From the 10th on you'll be committed to an exciting new project that will demand much of your time. The pressure may be high, but you'll find it stimulating.

The tennis tournament! It was certainly an "exciting new project"! I just hoped we would win.

Toward the end of the month concentrate on family matters. Don't neglect an old friend.

Randy? No, I wouldn't neglect him. I'd been writing. Maybe Ellen would come to visit. I skimmed through Ellen's horoscope, Leo, but it didn't say she might be traveling. Well, we'd see.

I'm not really a believer in these things, but it's strange the way my horoscope always seems to be right on target. Mom says it's only a coincidence, that you can read whatever you want into it, but I don't know. One time it said an unexpected gift would come my way and I won a camera in the school raffle. And last fall I got an A plus on an American History paper after it predicted that hard work would be rewarded. Who knows? Some things just can't be explained, but one thing was for sure. If there was anything to this astrology stuff, it sounded like Brad and I would be going strong. At least through the tournament.

I wanted him to call like he'd promised. We had the tennis competition to worry about and he had said himself that we couldn't take more than one or two days off from practice.

Just as I started paging through the rest of the magazine, the phone rang. On the third ring I picked up.

"Hello," I said casually, my heart thudding.

"Hi. I was beginning to think you weren't home."

"Oh, hi, Kim." I hoped she didn't notice my disappointment.

"Have you recovered from the barbecue?"

"Hardly. As a matter of fact I just got up. Did you have a good time with Mike?"

"Terrific. I can't believe he was a blind date and there was nothing wrong with him. They're usually such nerds."

43

"I know what you mean."

"He's going to be around for most of the summer."

"See, I told you it would be worth it."

"How about you? I didn't see much of you and Brad all night."

"Well, we took a walk along the beach and spent a lot of time talking."

"Talking?"

"Yes . . . well, among other things, that is."

"I thought so. I think you guys are going to be a major item before too long."

"So what do you want to do today?" I asked, quickly changing the subject.

"Maybe we can get a volleyball game going on the beach," Kim suggested.

"Okay. I'll meet you in about an hour."

As usual, I got to the beach before Kim. As I was spreading out my stuff I did a double take. Jenny was coming over. She was wearing one of her microscopic bikinis and, oddly, tennis shoes. Where was Kim when I needed her?

"Lauren, I was hoping I'd run into you this afternoon."

"What's up, Jenny?"

"Well, you probably know that Brad's birthday is next week."

I had no idea but didn't want to admit it. "Of course," I said firmly.

"Since he and I have been friends for such a long time," Jenny continued, "I've decided to throw a little party for him. Naturally I'd love to have you there."

Naturally, I thought to myself.

"And your friend too," she continued. "Uh, what's her name?"

"Kim."

"Right, Kim."

It's not that I didn't trust Jenny. Not really. It's just that she was being a little too nice, if you know what I mean.

"Sure, Jenny, I'd love to come. Is there anything I can do?"

"Let's see. No, I don't think so. But if something comes up, I'll let you know." She paused for a minute before she pounced. "By the way, I hear you and Brad have been playing tennis."

"Yeah, we've played tennis a couple of times," I hedged. "He's been helping me with the basics."

"Oh, then you wouldn't be entering the tournament, I suppose, would you?"

I decided to play dumb. "What tournament?" I asked, gazing at her blankly.

"You know, the Sea Gate tournament that Scott and I are . . . oh, never mind. It's not important. Gee, it's getting late. Oh, and remember, Brad's party is supposed to be a surprise, so don't slip."

"Don't worry. I won't breathe a word," I promised.

"See ya."

I lay back to soak up some serious sun. She seemed satisfied. It was hard to believe, but I must have convinced her I wasn't interested in the tournament. A dirty trick on my part, but I didn't want to give her the edge and let her know who she was up against. She'd find out soon enough. I closed my eyes.

"Hi there," said a voice above me.

I opened my eyes and sat up. It was Kim.

"Listen, I had a great idea." She sat down on my towel. "Let's go check out that deserted house Brad was talking about last night."

"Just the two of us?"

"Why not? I think it would be neat. You're not scared or anything, are you?"

"Me? Don't be silly," I fibbed.

"Good. Let's go."

"You'll never guess what," I said as we strolled along the water toward Sea Gate. "Jenny paid me a visit this afternoon."

"You're kidding. Here in Ocean Bluffs?"

"That's right."

"Lucky you. What was she doing, slumming or something?" Kim giggled.

"Get this. She invited us to a surprise party she's giving for Brad. His birthday's next week sometime."

"I'm honored, but how come she's giving him a party?"

"That's what I'd like to know. She said they've been good friends for a long time. What she really wanted was some information on the tennis tournament. Like whether or not Brad and I are entering."

"Now that sounds more like the Jenny we all know and love."

"She thinks she and her partner have the mixed doubles title all sewn up, and she's probably afraid of the competition," I guessed.

"You didn't tell her anything, did you?"

"Not a thing."

"Hey, speaking of Jenny," Kim said as we approached the Sea Gate Beach Club, "isn't that her playing tennis?"

I looked up at the courts. "I don't know. I can't see very well. Let's get closer."

We walked up to the dunes, and when we got a better look, my heart sank to my feet. That was Jenny all right. There she was, plain as day, volleying with Brad! My eyes filled up with tears. All of a sudden I turned away from Kim and started running back to Ocean Bluffs.

"Hey, wait for me," Kim called from behind.

I ran as fast as I could.

"Lauren!" Kim yelled. "Where are you going?"

She finally gave up. The sand was hurting my feet but I didn't care. All I wanted to do was go home.

I ran back to Ocean Bluffs, down Sandy Lane, and straight to the deck behind my house. I sat down on the chaise longue to catch my breath. Before long Kim appeared, looking concerned.

"Here, you left your stuff on the beach," she said, handing me my towel and magazine.

"Oh, thanks. I forgot."

"Will you quit being so upset? They were only playing tennis."

"I just couldn't stand seeing them together, Kim."

"I know. It's a drag. But Brad couldn't care less about Jenny."

"Oh, yeah? How do you know?"

"Just a hunch," Kim confessed.

"Oh, fine," I groaned.

"Look, he said he was going to call you, right?"

"Yes, but . . ."

"So then what are you worried about?"

"I don't know. I can't explain it."

"You're just suffering from a Jenny overdose. Twice in one day is more than the average person can handle. How about a double butterscotch sundae at Sprinkles? That should cure you."

"Thanks, Kim, but I'd rather hang out here."

"Okay, then I guess I'll see you tomorrow."

I moped around the house the rest of the afternoon. All through dinner I was pretty quiet, but no one seemed to notice. It was after eleven when I went up to my room. I sat on my bed playing solitaire and wondering why Brad hadn't called. Typical guy, I thought to myself, you never knew what they were thinking about. How could he play tennis with Jenny? I decided that her partner had probably dumped her and now she wanted to play in the tournament with Brad. I decided that I would have nothing more to do with Brad—or the dumb tournament.

At the same time I couldn't help wondering what Brad was doing. I was sure that he wasn't in his room playing solitaire and thinking about me. With all my heart I wished that I had never come to Fire Island. If I had been in Garden City, Randy and I would just about be coming out from a movie at this time. Or we would be at the Fireplace, or bowling. And I wouldn't be feeling so mad. So sad.

What a mess! I couldn't even sort out my own feelings! For the first time I began to understand some of the things Mom and Dad must have been feeling. They had been together for over six months now, but supposing they decided to call it quits again? I desperately wanted some kind of guarantee about Mom, about Dad, about Randy, about Brad, about just about everything.

After losing ten games of solitaire in a row—even when I cheated a little—I finally gave up and turned out the light. It was definitely not my lucky day. I closed my eyes but I still couldn't get Brad out of my head.

5

How come it's always for you?" Elizabeth complained, dropping the telephone receiver on the table.

"Who is it?" I whispered.

"How should I know?"

"Well, is it a guy?"

"Yeah, I think so."

Probably Brad, I thought. "Tell him I'm not here, Elizabeth, okay?"

"Tell him yourself," she snapped.

"Thanks a lot." She could be a royal pain when she wanted to. "Hello," I muttered into the receiver.

"Hi. I thought we'd get an early start on tennis this morning."

"Really? Well, you can just start without me, Brad."

"What do you mean?"

"You should be able to figure it out."

I slammed down the receiver. That should take care of him. I sat down on the sofa and picked up *The Fire Island News*. Within seconds the phone started to ring again. I just ignored it.

"Will somebody please get that?" Mom called from the kitchen.

"Hey, Elizabeth, I'll take you to the movies tonight if you answer the phone," I coaxed.

"It's a deal," she answered eagerly.

"If it's Brad tell him I'm out."

"Hello," Elizabeth said politely.

"Oh, hi, Brad," she went on. She looked over at me and nodded. "Lauren said if it was you to tell you that she's not here."

She certainly gets right to the point.

"How'd I do?" she asked as she hung up.

"Fine, Elizabeth. So what did he say?"

"Nothing. Just to tell you that he called. Do I get to pick the movie?"

"Huh? Oh, sure. Whatever you want."

I started reading *The Fire Island News* again and turned to the entertainment section. Elizabeth leaned over my shoulder to look at the listings. We were just discussing the merits of the new science fiction film, *Escape from the Fallen Planet,* when the doorbell rang. I sluggishly got up to answer it. I nearly froze when I saw who was at the door. Good old Brad, tennis racket in hand. He looked a little harried. I don't know how he did it, but he sure got over here in record time.

"What are you doing here?" I groaned.

"I was calling from the Ocean Bluffs courts," he

said, trying to catch his breath, "and I ran straight over. Are you going to let me in or do I have to talk to you through the screen?"

"Talk to me through the screen, if you must."

"Would you mind telling me what's going on?"

"I think you're the one who should be telling *me* what's going on, Brad."

"What are you talking about? All I did was call you up this morning for tennis practice, and the next thing I know you put Elizabeth on my case."

"I happened to be walking by the club yesterday and it looked as if you were getting more than enough tennis practice."

"Oh, so that's it. Listen, you've got it all wrong."

"I thought we were partners." I almost started to cry but I caught myself just in time.

"We are partners. Lauren, I don't want anyone on my team but you." He looked pretty funny as he pressed his face against the screen and squashed his nose. "Would you please open the door? I can't even see you through this thing."

I unlocked the door and he came in. "Then why were you playing tennis with Jenny?" I asked.

"Because she asked me and because I thought it wouldn't be a bad idea to see what kind of a game she played. You know, figure out where her weak spots are. Jenny and Scott are our only real competition, and I thought playing with her would help us plan our strategy."

"Oh, I didn't think of that," I said.

"By the way, her backhand's the pits, and if we hit to it we'll be home free."

"I feel pretty dumb," I admitted.

"Forget it. Just get your stuff. I booked court time."

I ran upstairs to get my racket. I was glad to take refuge in my room for a minute. Brad's story about checking up on Jenny's tennis sounded pretty good, but I couldn't help wondering whether or not he still liked her just a little.

I looked in the mirror and made a face at myself. "Well, I guess it's now or never," I said to myself. I grabbed my racket and went back downstairs.

Brad frowned as he glanced at his watch. "Let's go. We're late."

He was walking so fast I could hardly keep up with him.

"Listen, registration for the tournament opens tomorrow," he said. "Why don't you meet me at the club in the morning and we'll sign up first thing."

"Sure. When is the tournament, anyway?"

"End of July."

When we got to the courts, we sat down on the bench behind the fence. I clipped my hair back while Brad slid a sweatband over each wrist. He was acting as if nothing had happened, but I still felt pretty awful.

I looked over at him as he took his racket out of the press. "Brad, you know I'm really sorry," I said.

"I said forget it and I meant it." He moved closer and put both arms around me and kissed me. "Come on," he urged. "Let's play tennis."

He took both my hands and pulled me to my feet. Play tennis. He had to be kidding. Every time he kissed me I felt like fainting. I did my best to get my act together and took my place on my side of the court.

53

"We have to start working on our team positions," Brad explained. "Most of the time you'll be playing the net and I'll be in the back court. So stay up front and I'll hit a few balls over. I want you to perfect your forehand volley."

I stood at the net and returned each ball before the first bounce.

"You're doing great!" Brad yelled. "Keep it up."

After a few minutes he signaled for me to stop and I met him at center court.

"Now pretend I'm Jenny and hit to my backhand," he instructed.

"I don't have that much of an imagination."

"Then fake it." He laughed.

It took a while, but with Brad's patient coaching I finally learned to place the ball where it would be out of Jenny's reach. We practiced serving for a while and then we called it a day.

"We still have a few weeks before the tournament," Brad said, wiping his face with his towel. "It'll be close, but I think we can win. Like I said, if we just concentrate on Jenny's backhand, it shouldn't be too bad."

"By the way, what kind of player is Scott?" I asked.

"Unfortunately he's pretty good."

We gathered up our stuff and headed back to my house.

"Soon we should start practicing at the club so we can get the feel of the courts," Brad said.

"Let's start tomorrow after we register," I suggested.

"Now why didn't I think of that?" he said with a

smile. He paused for a moment and then looked over at me. "Incidentally, are you doing anything tonight?"

"Yeah, I'm busy. I promised Elizabeth I'd take her to the movies. We'll probably see *Escape from the Fallen Planet.*"

"That's too bad. I'd go along with you but I saw it last night with my little brother Billy. Pretty awful flick."

So that's why he didn't call, I thought.

"Hey, I know what we can do for a change," he went on. "Tomorrow night let's take the ferry over to the mainland. We can bum around Bay Shore and maybe see a *real* movie."

"I'd love to, Brad, but I don't know if my parents will go for it."

"Tell them I promise to have you home by midnight."

"Okay if I let you know tomorrow?"

"Sure."

I knew I'd have a hard time convincing them. First of all, they hardly knew Brad, and I doubted they would want me to leave the island. But sooner or later they'd have to realize that I wasn't a little kid anymore. After all, I'd never given them any reason not to trust me. Well, I'd give it a shot and see what happened. I just hoped that it wouldn't cause a big scene. The last thing I wanted was to mess things up.

"You'll really have your hands full tonight with that little sister of yours. She's something else. You know, I ought to introduce her to Billy."

"How old is he?"

"Ten and a half."

"Perfect. The two of them would get along great. Elizabeth is nine but very precocious."

"Yeah, so I noticed on the phone this morning."

I winced. I was trying to forget about that whole thing.

"I'll see you tomorrow morning at the club," Brad said as we stopped in front of my house. He quickly brushed his lips against mine. "Good luck with your parents."

"Thanks. I'll need it."

I watched him walk off. The thing about Brad was that he had a style all his own. No matter what he did, whether he was on the tennis court, at a party, or just hanging out, he always looked super-cool. A real asset for a future lawyer, but I wasn't so sure I wanted it in a boyfriend!

Brad was right. *Escape from the Fallen Planet* was awful. Kim and I barely managed to endure it, but Elizabeth's eyes were glued to the screen the whole time. Afterward we took the kid to Sprinkles for what Ellen would have called "the ultimate pig-out." We sat down at a cute round table and studied our menus.

" 'Chocolate Fantasy,' " I read out loud. " 'Chocolate-chocolate chip ice cream topped with chocolate syrup, walnuts, and whipped cream.' "

"You've talked me into it." Kim laughed. "Just call me Miss Piggy."

"Two Chocolate Fantasies, please," I said to the waitress when she came over to our table.

"I'd like a pistachio ice cream soda with extra whipped cream," Elizabeth said.

"Gross," I commented.

"Boy, that was the best movie I ever saw," Elizabeth exclaimed, still bubbling with enthusiasm. "I liked the part when the spaceship ran into the asteroids and everything blew up, didn't you?"

"Yeah, Elizabeth, it was really great," Kim answered sarcastically. She turned to me and continued. "I saw Mike today, Lauren, and he had a few things to say about Brad and Jenny."

"Such as what?"

"He said that two summers ago they were just about inseparable. Then something happened to break them up but Mike didn't seem to know what it was."

"Or maybe he didn't want to say."

"Perhaps. Anyway, last summer she tried her best to get him back."

"Apparently she hasn't given up." I scowled.

"Yeah, but you have nothing to worry about," Kim assured me as the waitress put three mountains of ice cream in front of us. "According to Mike, Brad thinks she's a pain in the neck."

"Are you sure?"

"Absolutely," Kim said, grinning. "He's just too polite to show it."

"Don't you guys ever talk about anything but boys?" Elizabeth asked.

"Quiet, Elizabeth. This is serious," I said. "I wonder if Brad has a girlfriend back home," I added, turning to Kim.

"Mike didn't say anything about that, but I can try to find out."

"What a bunch of junk," Elizabeth mumbled.

"Someday you'll understand, Elizabeth," Kim said knowingly.

"Not me," Elizabeth insisted.

"Elizabeth has decided not to go out with boys . . . ever," I explained.

"Oh, come on," Kim joked. "Just look at her. She'll probably be the heartthrob of the fifth grade."

Kim and I glanced at each other and cracked up while Elizabeth, with her blond braids falling around her shoulders, innocently sipped her pistachio soda.

Sometimes I wished it was as simple as Elizabeth made it sound. If I had just ignored boys altogether, I wouldn't have had any problems.

Brad and Randy were great, but life would have been a lot less confusing without one of them. The trouble was, I felt I had to choose, and I didn't know which one it should be. Brad was older and more sophisticated and all of that, but Randy was special, too, in his own way. We had always had such good times together. Well, I figured, two boys are better than none.

Mom had said that sometimes you have to do an awful lot of soul searching before you can sort out your feelings. I supposed that this was one of those situations. She said that she had done a lot of thinking when she and Dad had been separated. I guessed that Dad had done the same, only he hadn't talked about it. It was a lucky thing for me and Elizabeth that they had decided they still loved each other. I hated the idea of them ever divorcing. I really had to hand it to them. It must have been next to impossible to sort out things like love, commitment, and responsibility. Here I was a total wreck just trying to figure out which boyfriend I liked!

6

That morning at breakfast I wanted to ask Mom and Dad about going to Bay Shore with Brad, but I chickened out. Mom was in a terrible mood. Nothing would go right. She burned the toast. Elizabeth spilled her milk. Then two eggs rolled off the counter and splattered onto the floor. Fearless Schnapps decided to slide around in them a little. What a mess. He looked like a scrambled dog. It was definitely not the time to pop the question. I helped wash Schnapps off, but then I had to rush off to the club to meet Brad.

The time finally seemed right to drop the bomb. We had just finished lunch and Mom and Dad were lying on lounge chairs out on the deck. I casually strolled outside, hoping that I wasn't going to start World War III.

"What are you guys doing tonight?" I asked.

"We're playing bridge over at the Addisons'," Mom replied, never taking her eyes off her novel.

"Brad asked me to go to the movies."

"That's nice, dear," she said, half listening.

"The only problem is that we've both seen *Escape from the Fallen Planet*, so we'd like to go to one of the theaters in Bay Shore," I explained, hoping they'd take it in stride. But I had a feeling there would be an explosion any minute.

"On the mainland?" Dad said, raising his eyebrows. Mom put down her book.

"It's no big deal," I argued. "We'll take the ferry. Brad says it runs every half hour." I knew it was hopeless, but I figured I may as well state my case as long as I'd gone this far.

"I don't know, Lauren. I hardly know this Brad fellow," Dad responded.

"Oh, Dad, there's no reason to be concerned or anything. We just want to do something different for a change."

"I don't know," he repeated.

"He seems like a nice boy, Howard," Mom intervened. "I'm sure it'll be fine." I was glad she was on my side, but still, I felt kind of funny. I hated it when they disagreed over *me*.

"Well, I'm not crazy about the idea, but I suppose it'll be okay, just this once," Dad said. "As long as you're home early."

"Thanks." I dashed inside to call Brad. I could tell they were still discussing the situation, but I couldn't make out any words. Dad just had to get to know Brad a little better, that was all.

* * *

Brad wasn't picking me up until seven, so I had the afternoon all to myself. I wanted to look extra special for our date. I thought I'd condition my hair and give myself a manicure. My nails were a mess. I kept breaking them playing tennis.

I chuckled when I thought about registration for the tournament that morning. At first Jenny and Scott hadn't seen us. We had been standing in the line behind them. I had spotted Jenny right away.

Who could miss her? She was the only one there with pink pom-poms on her tennis socks. Jenny finally turned around, and for once she was absolutely speechless. Brad handled the situation with ease. He just smiled and said, "Hi, Jenny. We decided to enter at the last minute just for fun." Jenny just stood there with her mouth open.

I knew that winning the tournament was much more important to Brad than it was to me. He was really gung ho. Oh, it would be nice to win. But let's put it this way. If we lost, it wouldn't exactly ruin my summer. I was having a great time just being Brad's partner.

I still couldn't believe I was actually going out with him. I wished that just once the girls from Garden City High could see the two of us together. Regular old Lauren McDermott going out with a guy like Brad Caldwell! Boy, would they be in shock. I mean, let's face it, he was a hundred times cuter than anyone from home, not to mention that he was going to college in the fall. Wait until Ellen saw him. I'd been telling her about him in my letters, of course, but how could you describe a guy like Brad in words?

The afternoon dragged on and on. I thought seven o'clock would never come. I guess I spent most of the time getting ready for Brad. The hair conditioner worked pretty well. My hair came out really silky and shiny. Between the sun and the saltwater it had been in terrible shape. I did what I could with my emery board and nail buffer to save my disastrous nails. Then I figured as long as I was doing a complete overhaul, I may as well put some oatmeal mask on my face. Naturally Elizabeth came barging in the room and wanted to know why I didn't add milk and butter and have myself for breakfast. Kids!

I knew it would be chilly on the ferry, so I thought I'd wear the red cotton crew-neck sweater Mom had knitted for me last spring. It looked great over my blue and white pinstriped blouse. My best jeans had just been pressed. I had to struggle a little to get into them but it was worth it. They fit just right. As I studied myself in the mirror I decided that my hard work was worth it. I didn't look too bad after all.

I flew downstairs as soon as I heard the doorbell. By the time I got to the living room, Dad was already cross-examining Brad about our plans. I didn't mind, though. I knew Brad would put him at ease.

"You're taking Lauren to a movie tonight, Brad?" I heard Dad ask.

The minute I saw Brad, I felt butterflies in my stomach. He looked sensational in his khaki pants and white shirt. I must have been dreaming. Was I really going out with him?

"Yes, sir. I hope we can get in to see *Rebel in Disguise*," Brad explained. "We're going to the mainland because the Bay Shore Cinema's the only theater around that's showing it this summer."

"I've heard it's the hit of the season. It's supposed to be very funny," Mom said.

Brad's eyes met mine and we smiled. We were both surprised that Mom knew anything about it. Parents really fool you sometimes. "Yes," I chimed in. "I've been dying to see it."

"You know, Lauren, the lines for the movie could be brutal. I think we'd better get going if we're going to make that early ferry," Brad said.

I grabbed my navy blue windbreaker in case it rained or something. "I'm all set."

"Just be home by twelve, kids," Dad reminded us.

"No problem, Mr. McDermott," Brad assured him. "We're taking the eleven o'clock ferry back."

"Have a good time," Mom called as we made our way outside.

Dad still didn't look terribly pleased about the whole thing, but I knew Mom would take care of everything. At least I hoped so. I just wanted to have a good time and not worry about *anything*, including my parents.

The ferry didn't run out of Ocean Bluffs at night, so we were catching it at Ocean Beach. We took the usual route along Bay Walk. The thick, salty air felt heavy against my skin. There was a very fine mist in the air, but we could still see the outline of Bay Shore across the Great South Bay. Definitely frizz weather. I could practically feel my hair curling from the humidity. So much for hair conditioners.

"My father's a little uptight about our trip to Bay Shore, as you might have noticed," I commented.

"Yeah, well, like I said, it's really no big thing. People do it all the time." He paused for a second and then turned and looked at me. "Enough of that stuff. Did anyone ever tell you that you're the most beautiful girl on Fire Island? You look fantastic."

The most beautiful girl on Fire Island! No one had ever told me I was *the most beautiful girl* anywhere before. In fact, no one had ever told me I was *beautiful* at all.

Brad stopped suddenly. Then, right in the middle of Bay Walk, he took me by the shoulders, pulled me close to him, and kissed me. When we realized how silly we must have looked, kissing right there on the path, we both started to laugh.

It's hard to describe, but sharing that moment with Brad gave me such a warm feeling. I could tell by the way he looked at me that he felt it too. I seemed to be in a daze.

"Come on, Lauren, don't just stand there. We've got a boat to catch," Brad said, taking me by the hand.

When we got to Ocean Beach, a big blue and white boat, the *Sea Lion,* was already docked in the ferry slip. Brad bought our round-trip tickets and then we climbed up to the upper deck, where we'd have the best possible view. We sat back on the wooden benches and put our feet up on the white rail on the edge of the deck. We were both admiring the deep red sunset when Brad unexpectedly started chanting, "Red in the morning, sailor's warning. Red at night, sailor's delight."

I looked at him as if he were nuts. "What?"

"Oh, haven't you ever heard that?"

"No. Should I have?"

"I don't know. I thought everyone knew that expression."

"Not me. What does it mean, anyway?"

"If the sky's red at night that means the next day will be beautiful. You know, good for sailing. Sailor's delight. Get it?"

"Where'd you ever pick that up?"

"Who knows? But it looks like tomorrow will be a gorgeous day. It never fails."

"Whatever you say." My voice had a doubtful tone.

"You'll see," he said confidently. "Just stick with me."

"All aboard for Bay Shore," the first mate bellowed from the dock.

Brad put his arm around me and I leaned back against him, resting my head on his shoulder. The boat pulled slowly out of the slip and into the Great South Bay. We gradually picked up speed and Ocean Beach began to look smaller and smaller until it was hardly there at all. My hair was blowing wildly in the sea breeze. Frizz or no frizz, I didn't even care. Somehow it seemed as though Brad and I were doing something more exotic than just crossing the bay and going to a movie. I looked at him and pretended we were on his private yacht, sailing on the Mediterranean.

I was almost sorry when the half-hour ride was over. I could have sat up there on the deck with Brad all evening. When we filed off the boat, everything on the mainland looked kind of strange. I'd gotten used to the dirt paths, dune buggies, and Jeeps on

Fire Island. It was weird walking along paved streets and watching big cars speed by us.

The Bay Shore Cinema was right on Main Street. We couldn't believe the long line for *Rebel in Disguise*. It wound all the way around the corner.

"Look at this mess," Brad complained. "I knew it. I'll go get the tickets. Why don't you go get on the ticket holders' line and save us a place."

When we finally got in, we had to sit way up front. My neck got stiff from looking up at the screen, but I didn't mind. I hadn't laughed so hard since the time Ellen and I had to sing alto harmony together in music class.

I guess it was about ten twenty when *Rebel* ended and we left the theater. Everyone on the way out was still laughing.

"Listen, we have about a half hour to kill," Brad said. "Not a whole lot of time, but we should be able to find something to do."

"When did you say our ferry leaves?"

"Eleven. I know what we can do. Let's go to the Rusty Nail."

"Isn't that a bar?" I hesitated.

"Yeah. So?"

"I'm only seventeen, remember?"

"Oh, you mean you don't have any proof with you?"

"Uh, no, Brad, I don't."

"No problem. I know the guy at the door," he boasted.

"You know, I don't think we really have enough time. By the time we get there we'll have to leave. Maybe some other time, okay?"

"What's the matter, Lauren? You're with me. Nothing can happen. Besides, nobody would have to know about it but us, if that's what you're worried about."

"I'm not worried at all. I just don't feel like it, okay?"

"Whatever you say." He paused for a minute and then went on. "Maybe next week we can take the ferry over here again."

There was really nothing we could do then except walk over to the ferry. We'd be a few minutes early, but Brad said the boat usually got in ahead of schedule and we'd be able to board.

"That's funny. No boat," Brad said as we approached the dock. "I guess it's running a little late." He looked out over the water. "Strange. I don't see it coming. You can usually see it crossing the bay on the way in from Ocean Beach."

"Well, it's a little misty," I pointed out. "I'm sure it'll come into view soon."

"Yeah, I guess you're right."

We sat down on a bench and waited patiently for a few minutes. Ten forty-five. Ten fifty-five. But no sign of the boat.

"Hey, Brad, I hate to ask this, but how come we're the only ones waiting for the ferry?"

"You know, I was just wondering the same thing. This is weird. We'd better go check it out at the ticket office."

We got there just as the ticket agent, an old man with gray hair and wire-rimmed glasses, was closing up the booth.

"Excuse me, sir, but is the eleven o'clock ferry to Ocean Beach running late?" Brad asked.

"Eleven o'clock ferry? There's no eleven o'clock ferry."

Brad and I looked at each other with sheer horror.

"What do you mean? I've got a schedule right here." Brad fumbled through his pockets and produced the crumpled paper.

"Let me see that," the man said, wrinkling his brow. He took a look at the schedule and shook his head. "No, you must have read it wrong, son." He pointed to the timetable on the other side of the page. "You were looking at the weekend schedule. *This* is the one you should have been looking at. The Monday to Thursday schedule. See, there's no eleven o'clock ferry Monday to Thursday."

Brad looked as though he wanted to crawl under a rock. "Let's see, it's quarter past eleven now. When does the next one leave?"

"I'm afraid you missed the last boat."

"Missed it?" Brad said with disbelief.

My stomach was beginning to feel a little queasy.

"Yup. The last boat was at half past ten."

Now what? I wondered. I could just picture my parents watching the clock. They'd probably have the Coast Guard out at one minute past twelve. But worst of all, Dad would be really mad at Mom for convincing him to let me go in the first place.

"But we have to get back to Fire Island," Brad insisted.

"Well," the man said, "you could try Jimmy's water taxi service. There's a phone in the coffee shop across the parking lot. Let me warn you, they may not want to come all the way out here and pick you up this time of night, and if they do, it'll cost you, I can tell you that."

"Okay. Thanks a lot," Brad said.

Brad took my hand and we ran straight over to the coffee shop. It was empty except for a very tired looking waitress who was cleaning the counter. The phone was right up front, next to the window.

"Do you have a phone book?" I asked.

"Sorry, miss. You know how it is. They practically get up and walk out of here all by themselves."

"We have to get in touch with Jimmy's water taxi service," Brad explained. "It's an emergency."

"Oh, well, why didn't you say so? I've got their card right here." She opened a drawer full of junk and shuffled around until she finally fished it out. "Miss the last ferry?" she asked, handing Brad the card.

"Uh, yeah," Brad managed.

"Folks are doin' that all the time. Jimmy has some racket goin'," she muttered.

Wonderful, I said to myself.

Brad quickly dialed the number. "Hello? I need a water taxi from Bay Shore to Ocean Beach right away. . . . Forty-five minutes? Couldn't you get here sooner? Okay, then, forty-five minutes will be fine. How much is it? . . . Eight bucks a person! Hold on a minute." He put his hand over the mouthpiece. "How much money have you got on you?" he whispered to me.

I emptied my pockets. "Four fifty."

"I've got ten bucks. That's fourteen fifty. That'll just have to do. We'll bargain later."

Brad got back on the phone. "Can you pick us up at the Bay Shore ferry slip? . . . Two passengers. . . . My name is Caldwell. Brad Caldwell. Thanks. And hurry."

"I'd better call home and let my parents know we'll be late. They're going to kill me." I started to dial, but I abruptly hung up the receiver.

"What is it?" Brad asked.

"I just remembered something awful. They're not home. They're playing bridge over at the Addisons' and Elizabeth always goes with them."

"It doesn't really matter that much, does it?" Brad asked.

I couldn't believe he said that. "Are you kidding? Of course it matters. If I'm not home by twelve my parents will be furious." But that was only half of it. I didn't want to tell Brad that if my parents had a big fight over me, something terrible might happen. I didn't know what I'd do if Dad went away again.

"Don't tell me you might turn into a pumpkin or something," Brad teased.

"I don't think you're very funny, Brad."

"Sorry. It's just that my parents aren't like that."

"Don't they care?" I shot back.

"Sure they do," he insisted. "But they don't have to know what I'm doing every minute."

I took a deep breath. I didn't want to get even madder. It wasn't worth it. But I was beginning to think that Brad could be a little too cool once in a while, if you know what I mean.

I figured calling home was at least worth a try. I picked up the receiver and started to dial my number. On the sixth ring I gave up. "No answer. Maybe I can get the Addisons' number from Information."

I hung up and dialed 411. "Operator, could you tell me if you have a listing for Addison in Ocean Bluffs?"

"Sorry, no listing."

I turned to Brad and sighed. "No listing."

"That's what I figured," he said. "The phone is never in the summer family's name."

"Well, my parents have to get home sooner or later. I'll call back in a little while. When did you say the water taxi's coming? Forty-five minutes?"

"Yeah." Brad looked at his watch. "We should be home by one o'clock . . . if we're lucky."

"Do you want to call *your* folks?"

He shrugged his shoulders. "Nah. It doesn't matter. Let's go."

We walked across the parking lot and sat down on the bench again. I slipped my windbreaker on and pulled the collar up over my neck. The breeze from the bay made it feel more like fall than summer. Every so often Brad looked out over the water. We knew it was useless but we were both hoping the water taxi would be early. I was so restless I couldn't sit still. I got up and walked down to the dock. It was so dark I could hardly see.

I kept hoping that good fortune would be with me for once and that I would make it back before my parents got home. Then they would never know about the mix-up. I knew I was dreaming, but I kept hoping. Sometimes those bridge games went on and on. . . . But who was I kidding? I knew there wasn't a chance. I had finally convinced them to trust me and look what had happened. I could just see their reactions. I would never be allowed to take the ferry to Bay Shore again. Or, worse yet, they would never let me see Brad again. What would I do if that happened? The summer might just as well end.

I picked up a stone and tossed it into the bay.

Maybe I was jumping to conclusions. After all, Mom and Dad were reasonable people. We had a perfectly logical explanation, and Brad would probably be convincing. He always was. We'd simply tell them that we had read the schedule wrong. It happens all the time. But our excuse sounded shaky, even to me. I didn't even care if Mom and Dad were mad at me. I just didn't want anything to come between them again.

I wasn't exactly angry with Brad, but I didn't understand how he could have been so dumb. I mean, you'd think that someone going to Princeton would know how to read a ferry schedule. Even Elizabeth could have handled that.

I had that eerie feeling that someone was watching me, and when I turned around I nearly jumped out of my skin. Brad was standing right behind me.

"You scared me half to death," I gasped.

"Sorry. Hey, Lauren, I feel really awful about this whole thing. I think it's the dumbest thing I've ever done."

Yeah, it probably is, I said to myself. "Don't worry about it, Brad. It'll be all right."

"I just hope you won't have a hard time with your parents."

"That reminds me. I'd better try calling again."

We headed back to the coffee shop. It looked pretty quiet, but, thank goodness, it was still open. I immediately picked up the phone and started dialing. Brad went over to the waitress.

"Two hot chocolates to go," I heard him say.

I let the phone ring and ring. Darn. Where were they? It was twenty past twelve.

"Still no answer," I said to Brad as I hung up.

"Here." He handed me the hot chocolate. "It isn't much but it might help."

"Thanks."

We walked out front and leaned against the window, sipping our hot chocolate. We were both too tired to talk.

"Do you hear that?" Brad said excitedly.

I heard a faint humming in the distance. It sounded like an engine or something. "Is that our boat?" I wondered.

"Must be."

We dumped our hot chocolate in the nearest trash can and took off as fast as we could. We made it down to the dock just as the motorboat was pulling up.

"Are you Caldwell?" the skipper asked, puffing heavily on his pipe. He was wearing a captain's hat and an old navy blue jacket.

"Yes, sir, I called earlier."

"That'll be sixteen dollars, please."

Brad scraped together our money and handed it over.

The skipper painstakingly counted it. "There's only fourteen fifty here," he grumbled.

"Yes, sir. I know we're a little short. But I promise I'll bring the rest to you tomorrow. We're really in a rush to get back to Fire Island," Brad pleaded.

The skipper took one look at my panic-stricken face and mellowed. "Forget it. We'll call it even. Hop in."

There was room for about eight people or so, but we were the only passengers. We sat down on the side behind the skipper. Once the boat picked up speed it started to get pretty cold and windy. Every so often our faces were sprayed with ice-cold water. I didn't mind, though. I was relieved that we were finally on our way home.

"There's an old army blanket under the back seat if you kids get cold," the skipper yelled. Between the wind and the noise from the engine it was hard to hear.

Brad leaned over and pulled it out of the compartment. We wrapped it around ourselves and huddled together.

"We'll have to run all the way from Ocean Beach to Ocean Bluffs," I sighed.

"Are you kids goin' to Ocean Bluffs?" the skipper asked over his shoulder.

"Yes, sir," Brad answered.

"You should've told me. I can take you directly there if you'd like."

Brad practically jumped overboard. "Fantastic! I didn't even know you went that far east."

"You kiddin'? Jimmy's taxi goes anywhere. If the price is right, that is."

Brad and I looked at each other and smiled. The old skipper was really a character.

"You wouldn't by any chance be Jimmy, would you?" Brad asked.

"You guessed it."

"Hey, Jimmy," I asked sheepishly, "you've got plenty of gas and all that, right?"

"Plenty of gas. Don't you worry, miss. This little boat is shipshape."

Whew. I'd been afraid to ask. I had visions of us running out of gas or, worse, of the engine conking out in the middle of the bay. If I wasn't with Brad I'd be scared to death.

"Yessiree," the skipper went on, "I've been travelin' these waters for years and years now. Never had a problem."

Little did he know he had Lauren McDermott, national disaster and the biggest jinx in the western world, aboard. The way my luck was running, I shuddered when I thought about all the things that could go wrong. Better not to think about it, I decided.

We cruised across the bay in record time. Jimmy was certainly much faster than the ferry.

"Thanks for everything," Brad said to Jimmy as we pulled into the dock in Ocean Bluffs.

"Anytime," Jimmy said, grinning. "Glad to help you kids out."

Brad and I climbed up onto the dock and then ran as fast as we could along Bay Walk. I could see A Summer Place from the corner as we turned down Sandy Lane. All the lights were on. Bad sign. They must be home.

Brad kissed me good night out front.

"Well, I guess this is it. Good luck," he said.

"You're going right home?" I was shocked.

"Yeah, you know it's going to be later than I thought by the time I get back to Sea Gate. I'll see you at tennis practice tomorrow."

I couldn't believe he wasn't coming in with me. How could he just throw me to the wolves like that? I had kind of an empty feeling inside. I felt he had really let me down.

"Yeah," I said softly, "I guess I'll see you tomorrow."

When I finally mustered up enough nerve to go in the house, Mom was sitting on the sofa and Dad was wearing a hole in the carpet from pacing back and forth.

"Lauren!" Mom cried, springing to her feet. "We've been worried sick. Thank goodness you're home."

"Where on earth have you been? It's after one," Dad asked in a soft monotone. I knew I was in for it. When he was *really* angry he never raised his voice. He just sort of muttered through clenched teeth. Schnapps had the right idea. He sneaked off into the corner and curled up in his bed.

"It's kind of a long story," I said timidly.

I could see old Elizabeth peeking out from behind our door upstairs. She didn't miss a thing. I'd take care of her later.

I went on about the ferry schedule, the man in the ticket booth, the telephone calls, and Jimmy. The story was so ridiculous it had to be true. Who could make up anything so crazy?

"Do you have any idea how concerned we were?" Dad hadn't stopped pacing yet, and he was still yelling in his near-whisper.

"Of course I do, Dad. That's why I tried calling so many times. I even tried to get the Addisons' number, but it's not listed."

"I told you, Anne," Dad went on. "I just didn't feel right about this whole thing."

"It sounds like it was an honest mistake, Howard."

"It really wasn't my fault, Dad. We did everything we could."

"Maybe you should choose your friends a little more carefully," he advised sharply.

"It won't happen again, Dad. I promise."

"It better not," he said sternly.

"I think we could all use some sleep." Mom sighed.

Amen. I slipped upstairs as inconspicuously as possible. I could tell that Mom and Dad weren't going to say anything more on the subject until I was out of the way.

Elizabeth was doing her imitation snore when I walked into our room. "Don't bother, Elizabeth. I know you're awake. How come you're such a little busybody?"

"I didn't want to miss anything good." She yawned.

"Well, you didn't."

"Did you get in trouble?"

"None of your business."

"I'll bet you did."

"Good night, Elizabeth."

As I changed into my nightshirt I could hear their voices echoing up the stairs. From the sounds of things they were still disagreeing about whether or not I should have gone to Bay Shore in the first place. I cupped my hands over my ears and buried my head in my pillow. I just didn't want to hear any more.

7

Holy crackers! You've got to be kidding!"

"It's the gospel truth, Kim. Every word. I promise you."

We were sitting on the floor in Kim's living room, leaning against her bed. I was telling her all about the night before while our favorite rock station, WFVF-FM, played in the background.

"Holy crackers!" she repeated, shaking her head. "Lydia would have hit the roof. Did they tell you that you couldn't see Brad anymore?"

"No. Dad made it pretty clear that he's not too thrilled about Brad, but they're leaving the whole thing up to me."

"Sounds like you got off pretty easy."

"I haven't told you the worst of it yet."

"You're kidding. There's more?"

"Listen, I have to absolutely swear you to secrecy.

I've never discussed this with anyone but Randy and Ellen."

"You can count on me to keep a secret, Lauren. You know that."

"Okay. Here goes." I sighed heavily. I hated to talk about it. "Last year my parents split up for about six months. It was the worst. Dad lived in New York and Elizabeth and I stayed in Garden City with Mom. Then, just before Thanksgiving, they decided to give it a go again. Things have been working out pretty well."

"You're lucky they got back together. I kept wishing my parents would do that after they first separated. So what's the problem?"

"The thing is, sometimes I feel like I'm walking on eggshells. I'm scared to death I'm going to do something to spoil everything. Like last night."

"Oh, Lauren, that's ridiculous."

"No. You don't understand. Last night I could hear them arguing after I went to bed. I know they were fighting about Brad and me. I've been thinking. Maybe I *should* stop seeing Brad."

"That's the dumbest thing I've ever heard. Look, you can't blame yourself. If your parents have problems between themselves, that's something else. Not seeing Brad won't change anything. Besides, you didn't do anything wrong. The whole thing was just a big mix-up."

"I know, but if I hadn't gone to Bay Shore in the first place, my parents never would have had the argument."

"Well, maybe eventually they would have quarreled over something else. Parents have differences of opinion all the time, but that doesn't mean they're going to get divorced over every little thing. I kind of know how you feel, though. At first I thought my parents were getting divorced because of me, but they both assured me I had nothing to do with it. Believe me, if you blame yourself, you'll really mess yourself up. Why don't you talk to your mom or something?"

"Yeah. I guess I should."

"My dad always says you should never jump to conclusions. You said your parents worked everything out, and there's no reason to believe anything's changed, right?"

"Right. Thanks, Kim. I thought you might think I was nuts or something."

"I've been there and I know it isn't fun. There's only one thing I don't understand," she went on, looking rather puzzled.

"What's that?"

"Well, I'm kind of surprised that Brad didn't help you explain things to your parents."

"He hardly knows them," I said quickly. "He probably thought it was better for me to face them alone. He might have just made it worse." But the truth of the matter was that this bothered me too. Brad hadn't even offered to come in with me. I kind of felt he should have. After all, the whole thing had really been his fault. I didn't want to admit this to Kim, though. I had the feeling that she didn't really like Brad anyway, and I didn't want to have her dislike him all the more.

"I would've been scared to death," Kim said.

"I was."

"How come nothing exciting ever happens to me? You know what I did last night? Mike came over and we watched TV."

"Lucky you. When I heard we'd missed the last ferry, I'd have given anything to be safe and sound in my living room watching TV."

"Wait a minute," she said, grinning. "We did have some excitement. Mike decided to go into the kitchen and make popcorn. I assumed he knew what he was doing. The only problem was that he didn't know you're supposed to cover the pan."

"Oh, brother," I groaned. "Didn't he read the directions?"

"I guess not. I ran into the kitchen and popcorn was flying all over the place. Mike was trying to catch it. What a riot!" Kim and I couldn't stop laughing. "I lunged for the lid and covered the pan before too much damage was done."

"That's too much. You know, guys can be really dangerous."

"You're right. They just can't be trusted with ferry schedules or popcorn." Kim laughed.

"For sure," I agreed.

Kim got up and made the radio a little louder. Our favorite song was on.

"You know, Lauren, I did a little investigating for you." She grabbed a couple of pillows and tossed one over to me.

"What kind of investigating?" I asked.

"About Brad's love life. I finally got Mike to talk."

"Anything good?"

"Well, I got some information, but I don't know for sure how good it is."

"So spill it, will you, Kim?"

"Let me warn you. It might not be exactly what you want to hear."

"I don't care. I want to know anyway."

"Okay then, here goes. Mike said that Brad has a regular girlfriend back home."

Her words pierced right through me. "What do you mean by regular?" I choked.

"You know, they've been going out for a couple of years."

"Steady?"

"Sort of. But not really. Brad goes out with other girls too. Let's face it. He just doesn't seem like the steady type."

"What's her name?"

"I think it's Catherine."

Catherine. Even the name was pretty. "Well, do you know anything about her?"

"Not a whole lot. Mike said they were in the same class in school and she was a cheerleader."

"Oh, is that all," I said sarcastically. "That figures. She was probably only the most popular girl in school and gorgeous." I could feel the jealous streak in me coming to the surface fast. I wanted to know all there was to know about Catherine. The color of her eyes, the color of her hair, how tall she was. Everything. But how could I find out? "I know I don't have any right to be jealous, but . . ."

"You're right. You don't," Kim said quickly. "Don't even think about her. They're both going away to college in the fall. He'll be in New Jersey and she'll be out West. Who knows what'll happen?"

"That's another thing," I complained. "I don't know if I'll ever see Brad again after this summer."

"Has he dropped any hints?"

"Not really."

"Maybe he'll invite you to Princeton for a weekend or something."

"Are you kidding? Even if he did, my parents would never let me go."

"He'll have to come home once in a while. He doesn't live that far from you, does he?"

"No, not very far. I guess there's hope. Sometimes I wish I knew exactly where I stood with him. Who knows? I may just be another summer fling."

"I kind of know what you mean," Kim said. "Sometimes I get the impression that he thinks he's Mr. Cool. You know, like all the girls are supposed to be at his feet. I hope you don't mind my saying so."

"No, not at all." Maybe I minded a little, but it was okay.

"Maybe you could ask him how he feels about you," Kim suggested.

"Oh, sure. Just walk right up to him and blurt it out. 'Hey, Brad, am I just a summer girlfriend or are you really serious about this?'"

"Oh, come on, Lauren. Of course you can't do that. But you could ask him indirectly. I'm sure you can manage."

I was beginning to get a headache. "You know, Kim, it gets so confusing. When I start to think that I might like to see Brad after the summer's over, I begin to wonder about Randy. I really like Randy, too, and I don't want to give him up. I mean, I couldn't possibly imagine being without Randy."

"I should have such problems. Two boyfriends. That'll be the day," Kim lamented.

"It isn't always a whole lot of fun."

"By the way, have you heard from Randy lately?"

"No. Not for a couple of days. I should be getting a letter soon." I suddenly had a terrible thought. "Unless, of course, he's found someone else. For all I know he may never want to see me again."

"Now you're starting to sound crazy. From what you've said about Randy, I doubt that'll happen."

Probably not, I thought. But then, as Mom always said, sometimes you lose things when you start taking them for granted. What I really had to do, I decided, was to find out how serious Brad really was, and then I could make up my mind between him and Randy. I'd just have to decide once and for all. Right now I wanted to forget the whole business. I wanted to think about nothing more complicated than tennis practice.

"I hope I run into Jenny over at the club today," I said, changing the subject.

Kim looked shocked. "That's a switch. Since when do you want to see Jenny?"

"I have to get the details on her party for Brad. I don't even know when it is."

"Oh, Mike said Brad's birthday is next Thursday. So that's probably when the party is."

"You're a regular Sherlock Holmes."

"What are friends for?"

"Let's see. Next Thursday is the seventh," I calculated. "That would make Brad a Cancer. I wonder what that means."

"Let's check it out. I'll get my astrology book." Kim rummaged through a bunch of books on her night table shelf.

The seventh. I remembered my horoscope from

Harper's. It said something like "A new romance in your life may get complicated after the seventh." Weird. I began to wonder if something would happen at Jenny's party.

"Are you really into that astrology stuff?" I asked.

"Not really. I just dabble a little. How about you?"

"I read my horoscope in a magazine every month, but that's all."

"Here it is. *Star Guide*. I'll look up Cancer." She flipped through the pages. "Cancer," she read. "They list some characteristics. Confident. Warm. Magnetic personality. Charming. Intelligent. Keen intuition. Impulsive. Sometimes oversensitive. Unstable in love."

"That sounds like Brad all right."

"Best mate for Cancer is Taurus. What's your sign?"

"Aries." Catherine is probably a Taurus, I thought.

"Oh, well. This stuff doesn't really mean anything, anyway," she said, placing the book back on the shelf. "By the way, are you going to get Brad a present?"

"I hadn't even thought of that. I guess so. I don't have the slightest idea what to get."

"How about a new record album?" Kim suggested.

"That's a possibility." I looked at my watch. Time to leave for the club. "I'd better get going. I don't want to keep my coach waiting."

"I'll walk you outside." Kim led the way.

On my way to the club I noticed the clear blue sky

and the brilliant sunshine. Brad's weather prediction last night had been right. Red at night, sailor's delight. I'd have to remember that.

I decided I wouldn't mention the night before's big mess to Brad. What was the point? If he wanted to talk about it, fine. I just didn't understand why he wasn't more concerned. I could have gotten in a lot of trouble. I could tell that Kim thought he'd acted pretty weird too. I was almost positive she pretended to like him only because I did. I guessed he just wasn't her type.

I climbed the big stone steps up to the club. Lots of people were lying in the sun on the patio or sitting on the terrace by the pool. The tennis courts were pretty crowded, but I could see that court seven was empty. That was the one Brad had booked for us. I hurried up.

I decided to leave my yellow canvas bag in the locker room. I'd brought along my swimsuit in case we felt like taking a dip after practice. I tossed my bag into an empty locker, and I was about to head out to the courts when Jenny cornered me. She had obviously just finished playing a few games herself. She was sweating and her hair was all messed up.

"You look like you've had a pretty good workout," I said.

"Scott and I always get a good workout on the courts. You know, you'll need a lot of practice, too, if you think you'll ever come close to the finals."

"Don't worry, Jenny. We've been working hard. And Brad's a good teacher."

"Yes, I know."

I let that one go right by me. "You know, I've

been meaning to ask you. Exactly when is your party for Brad, anyway?"

"On his birthday, of course," she snapped. "Next Thursday."

"Oh, right. That's what I thought. Just wanted to be sure."

"Would you mind bringing something? Maybe a bottle or some beer?"

"Sorry, Jenny, but I'm not eighteen. I've heard the liquor stores on the island are really strict."

"Oh, I'm sure you'll find a way, Lauren. You're very resourceful."

"How about if I make fudge brownies instead? I have a terrific recipe from my grandmother." When I saw the disgusted look on Jenny's face, I realized how ridiculous that must have sounded to her. There was a silence that seemed to last forever.

She stared at me blankly. "Okay," she finally said. "I'll get one of the older kids to take care of the serious stuff."

It was definitely time to make my exit. "I'd better get out to the courts. I don't want to be late." I grabbed my racket and whizzed by her. She must have thought I was the biggest nerd in the world. But who cared, anyway? There was no way I could have brought beer or anything to her stupid party.

"Hi," Brad said. "I was ready to send a search party into the locker room."

"Very funny. I was talking to Jenny."

A tall figure in the next court caught Brad's eye. "Hey, speaking of Jenny, there's her partner, Scott Harrington, across the court."

I took a good look. I had to admit he was pretty

cute. Blond, like Brad, but he didn't have that little-boy charm that made Brad so adorable. He was running around the court making all the spectacular shots, and then in between kind of grinning in a self-conscious way.

"He looks kind of conceited," I commented.

"You've got it. Hey, I almost forgot. How'd you do with your parents last night?"

Almost forgot! I nearly got grounded for the rest of my life and he almost forgot! "Oh, it was nothing," I lied. "They took it fine."

"See, I told you it would be okay. Come on. Let's get to work."

I think I must have still been a little angry about the night before because I couldn't hit the ball. Things Kim said kept popping into my head. Like "Don't blame yourself" and "Your parents' problems aren't your fault." It was almost impossible to concentrate, and to make matters worse, Brad was making me run all over the court. I missed a basic forehand volley and then nearly fell over trying to return a tough backhand.

"What's with you?" I yelled across the net as I picked up the ball. "Are you trying to wear me out?" No way was I going to tell him about my parents or that I was pretty peeved at him.

"What's with *you?*" he shot back sharply. "You should be able to hit these balls easily." He was really annoyed. "This is nothing compared to the way you'll have to run around in the tournament games. Now stand at the baseline and keep your racket back and your head up."

Racket back, head up. I was doing my best. I

89

figured I was playing a little better than before, but I still missed a couple of easy shots. Brad didn't look happy. The clincher came when I hit the ball right into the path of the player on the next court, disrupting his game.

"Let's take a break," Brad called.

We met at the bench on the side of the court. Brad threw a towel around his neck and dried his face and hair.

"Look, Lauren, you're not even trying. I know you can do better. You're not psyching yourself. Every time you get out there you've got to pretend you're playing for the women's singles title at Wimbledon. The championship game. Every point is crucial. Who knows? You could be the next Tracy Austin."

"Wimbledon?" The closest I'd ever get to that famous English tournament would be watching it on television.

"That's right. Winning is a state of mind. It's all in your head."

"Okay, if you say so. I'll think Wimbledon."

"Great. That'll be our team motto from now on. Think Wimbledon. I like that. Let's get back out there. And I want to see some real tennis."

"Okay, coach."

I felt a little silly. Think Wimbledon. Well, I decided, Brad's method was at least worth a try.

We played a few games and you know what? I almost beat Brad for the first time ever. Then I helped him practice his backhand for a while before we quit.

"Hey, McDermott," Brad joked as we walked off the courts. "When I told you to get your act together before, I didn't mean you should practically kill me."

"Sorry," I said. "I couldn't help myself. I was just doing what you said. You know, thinking Wimbledon."

"I think I've created a monster."

He was flashing his famous smile again. It was impossible to stay mad at him. Even if he had acted like a jerk the night before, he was still adorable.

"How about a swim before lunch?" he asked.

"Great." I went back into the locker room to change into my swimsuit.

Brad was already on the diving board when I got down to the pool. He did a perfect jackknife and then swam a couple of laps when he surfaced. I dove in from the side and joined him. We had a great time splashing around.

"Have you ever been kissed underwater?" Brad asked.

"No," I said breathlessly.

"Want to try?" he said with a smile.

"Why not?"

We both took a deep breath and plunged under. I couldn't see a thing. I've never been able to open my eyes underwater. But Brad found me, and before I knew it he put his arms around my neck and kissed me. It was so strange. Suddenly all I could think of was Randy. I couldn't hold my breath any longer so I pushed away and swam to the surface. Brad came up right after me.

"What's the matter? Run out of air?" he asked, laughing.

"I guess I'd make a crummy mermaid." I splashed some water in his face.

He splashed me back. "Come on. Let's have lunch before we get completely waterlogged."

The nice thing about the club was that it was such a casual place. It was really elegant and all that, but if you wanted to have lunch on the patio in your swimsuit, nobody cared. We sat down at a table in the corner so we'd have a clear view of the ocean. Brad and I always had the same thing. The waiter brought a chicken salad sandwich and iced tea for me and a bacon cheeseburger, French fries, and a Coke for Brad. There were a million things I wanted to know about the tournament, and I figured now was as good a time as any to ask.

"How many couples are entering the mixed doubles competition?" I asked as I stirred my iced tea.

"The club limits the competition to sixteen couples. There are two divisions. Eight couples in each," Brad explained. "Would you pass the ketchup?" he added.

I set the bottle down next to him. "So how many times will we actually have to play?"

"We'll keep on going as long as we keep winning. If we lose the first match we're out, but if we win, and keep on winning, we could play a maximum of four times. There are the preliminaries, quarterfinals, semifinals, and then the finals."

"That doesn't sound too bad." I was watching him eat his French fries. He always made a little pool of ketchup and then dipped each French fry into it, one by one. I just dump the ketchup over the whole bunch. Much easier. Some day I'd have to ask him why he did it that way.

"Don't be fooled," he cautioned, carefully dipping a fry. "After the prelims it gets much more difficult."

"When do we play Jenny and Scott?"

"They're in a different division than us, so we won't play them at all unless we both make the finals. If we do, then we'll play them for the championship."

"That'll be tough. Do you want my pickles?" I asked.

"Sweet or dill?"

"Sweet, I think."

"No thanks. I have a funny feeling that's what's going to happen. We'll probably play Jenny and Scott in the finals, and it won't be easy. I was watching Scott on the courts today. Awesome."

"Really?" I sounded discouraged.

"Don't worry. We'll psych 'em out."

"Right. They don't know about thinking Wimbledon."

The waiter dropped off the check and Brad quickly signed it.

"I've got to split," he said apologetically. "I promised I'd help Billy practice softball."

"More coaching?"

"Yeah. Billy's in the Fire Island Little League. You'll have to come to the game when Sea Gate plays Ocean Bluffs."

"Wouldn't miss it. I should be going too. I have to write some letters." What I meant was I hoped there would be some letters waiting for me. Especially a letter from Randy.

Mom was hanging some wet bathing suits out on the line when I walked around back to the deck.

"Hi. How was practice?" she called.

"The usual."

"There are a couple of letters for you inside."

"Thanks." I hurried into the kitchen and immediately recognized the familiar handwriting on the envelopes. Randy and Ellen. I decided to open Ellen's letter first and save the best for last. I sat down at the table and started reading.

Dear Lauren,

I have to make this brief. Tom is picking me up and we're going to a free concert in Eisenhower Park. Guess what? My parents said I could come out to Fire Island for a couple of days during the last week in July. Isn't that fantastic?

Great! Just like my horoscope said. This means she'll be here for the tournament, I thought.

Why don't you check it out with your folks and let me know what dates are good, okay? I can hardly wait. I'm dying to see Fire Island. From what you've said about it, it sounds terrific. And Brad must be a real hunk.

By the way, Randy looks great. I ran into him at Joni Hartman's party last week. He has a real good tan from working at the pool. I guess being a lifeguard agrees with him.

Well, more later. Tom will be here any minute. Hurry up and write and let me know when I can come.

Adios,
El

I found Ellen's letter disturbing. I guess Randy can go to parties if he wants to, I thought. After all, I've practically got another boyfriend. What would Randy say if he knew that? I was sure he would be hurt. But I couldn't help it. Perhaps he would never find out. One thing was sure. It would be good to have Ellen visiting me. I could really talk to her. She was about the only person who would really understand.

I was anxious to see what Randy had to say. I hadn't heard from him in four whole days. I was beginning to think he'd forgotten about me. I tore open his letter.

Dear Laur,
    I can't believe it's July already. Summer is really flying by. The Garden City pool has been packed lately. All the guards have been working like crazy. It'll really pay off. I've put in so much overtime. I've just had a day or two off here and there, but I'm hoping to get a weekend off toward the end of the season so I can come out to visit you.

It would be great to see Randy, but what would I do with Brad? I decided to cross that bridge when I came to it.

    All in all, it's been a pretty quiet summer so far. Of course, I miss you like crazy. There's no one to hang out with. The Fireplace just isn't the same without you. I can't wait until summer's over and we can start going out like we used to. I won't even mind being in school.

See you soon. Have fun.

Love,
Randy

Randy could be so sweet. I missed him a whole lot, too, especially when I thought about all the good times we'd had together. It seemed funny, though, that he hadn't said anything about Joni Hartman's party. Maybe he'd had a rotten time and figured it wasn't even worth mentioning. Or maybe he had had a great time and didn't want me to know about it. I'd have to get the whole scoop from Ellen.

I was still sitting at the kitchen table reading my letters when Mom came in. She pulled up a chair next to me. "Who did you hear from?" she asked.

"Ellen and Randy."

"What's new back home?"

"Good news from Ellen. Her parents said she can come out for a couple of days sometime during the last week in July. Is that okay?"

"That's fine."

"When should she come?"

Mom took a look at the calendar hanging on the wall. "How about the twenty-sixth to the twenty-seventh. Monday and Tuesday?"

"Great. She'll get to see part of the tournament. I'll let her know right away."

"How's Randy?" Mom asked.

"Okay, I guess."

"He's a nice boy."

"Yeah. Randy's great."

"You don't sound as enthusiastic as you used to. I

remember a time—just a month ago, in fact—when Randy was all you ever talked about. You hardly ever mention him anymore."

"I know. But I still like him. I guess Brad's been keeping me pretty busy since we got to Fire Island."

Mom seemed to be reading a lot into what I said. "Just remember, dear, Brad will be going off to college in the fall. It might not be a good idea to get too attached to him. And it isn't fair to string Randy along if you're not planning to go out with him anymore."

Mothers! Why do they have to lecture all the time? "Oh, I still want to go out with Randy," I said. "But Brad's so different from all the guys at home. He seems more sure of himself . . . more sophisticated." Privately I was thinking, "and more *experienced,*" but I could hardly tell my mother how I felt whenever he kissed me.

"I just don't want you to get hurt, Lauren."

I've got news for you, I said to myself. I don't want to see me get hurt either.

"Is Dad still really angry about last night? I mean, you don't mind if I still go out with Brad, do you?"

"Your father and I talked things over and we decided you're certainly old enough to make your own decisions."

Sometimes, I thought, it would be easier if someone else made my decisions for me.

I hesitated a little, but I just had to ask. "Everything's still okay with you guys, right?"

"What do you mean, Lauren?"

"You know . . . between you and Dad."

Mom leaned over and put her arm around my shoulder. "Of course, Lauren. I thought we'd gone over all that months ago. Dad and I have worked things out. You know that."

"I just wanted to be sure, that's all. I think I'll go upstairs and write to Randy and El."

"Dinner will be ready around six," she called as I headed for my room.

Elizabeth was reading a Nancy Drew mystery. Good. She should stay pretty quiet. Sometimes I wondered if Elizabeth worried about Mom and Dad as much as I did. She never said much. I sat down on my bed, took out my stationery, and began to write. Ellen first. She'd be easier.

Dear El,

    I checked it out and Mom said that the best time for you to come would be the twenty-sixth and the twenty-seventh. That's a Monday and Tuesday. I can't wait to see you. It feels like it's been ages.

    I know you'll like all the kids here. Especially Kim. I've told you about her. She's moving to Port Washington in the fall. Incidentally, Brad *is* a hunk. You'll like him too.

    I got a letter from Randy and he says he might be able to come out for a weekend at the end of the summer. That'll be great, but I've got to talk to you about it when you get here. See ya soon.

Love,
Lauren

As soon as I finished addressing the envelope I remembered the tournament. Darn. I'd already sealed it. I turned it over and wrote one last message on the flap.

    P.S. I forgot to tell you. You'll be able to see Brad and me play in the tournament while you're here. I'll save you a ringside seat.

I looked at Randy's letter again. I had no idea what I would say to him, but whatever it was, I wanted it to be good. I wanted him to know that I still liked him.

"Lauren, Brad's on the phone," Dad yelled from the bottom of the stairs.

"Be right there."

I put Randy's letter aside. I would write him later when I had thought about it more. After all, there was really no hurry.

8

"Can I help?"

"Not a chance, Elizabeth."

I knew better. If you let Elizabeth help you in the kitchen, you're really asking for trouble. Everything she touches turns into a disaster. Believe me, I've learned the hard way.

"Please," she begged.

"Oh, at least let her watch," Kim coaxed.

Kim had come over to help me bake brownies for Jenny's party.

"Are you crazy?" I cried.

"How much damage could she do, Lauren? She's just a little kid."

"Just a little kid? That's like saying just an atomic bomb!"

"Oh, come on. She couldn't be worse than Mike and his popcorn fiasco."

"That's what you think," I said under my breath. But against my better judgment, I finally gave in. "Okay, Elizabeth," I conceded. "You can watch. As long as you stay out of the way."

Elizabeth knew she was treading on thin ice. She tiptoed over to the kitchen table and quietly sat down.

"You may live to regret this, Kim," I warned.

"What are you making?" Elizabeth asked.

"Chocolate fudge brownies," I replied. "If we ever find the pans, that is." Kim and I had practically turned the whole kitchen upside down looking for them.

"Like Grandma Adams makes?" Elizabeth's eyes lit up.

"Yup. We're using her recipe."

"Oh, boy. They're my favorite."

"If you're good you can have one," I promised.

"What are you going to do with the rest of them?"

"They're for Brad's birthday party, Elizabeth, so don't make any plans for them."

"Can I come?"

"Absolutely not."

"Hey, guess what? I found the pans!" Kim yelled. She pulled them out of the oven. "That's a pretty weird place for them."

"Oh, yeah. I forgot. Mom stores stuff in the oven if she runs out of room in the cabinets. Will you preheat it to three fifty while you're over there?"

I skimmed the recipe and then handed it to Kim. "Here, why don't you read me the ingredients and I'll get them out."

"Okay. Here goes." She began reading them off.

"Sugar. Flour. Baking powder. Chopped walnuts. Unsweetened chocolate . . ."

"Got it."

"Just a few more things. Salt. Four eggs. Butter. That's it."

"We may as well get started."

Kim placed the saucepan on the burner. We melted a cup of butter with four squares of unsweetened chocolate. I checked the recipe again. "Now we have to add in two cups of sugar, four eggs, two cups of flour, two teaspoons of baking powder, and a dash of vanilla. I'll stir and you toss everything in."

Kim poured in the sugar, flour, and baking powder and added the eggs. Then she picked up the vanilla and looked kind of blank. "How much is a dash?"

"Just a little. You know, a splash. Grandma Adams isn't very fussy."

"At least it looks like brownie batter," she observed. "That's everything except for the walnuts." Kim stuck her finger into the saucepan and tasted the mixture. "Not bad," she commented. "It tastes like brownie batter, too. Well," she added, "it's all up to Mike now. He has to get Brad over to Jenny's without giving away the surprise."

"Poor Mike. I could never do that. I've been on edge all week. I was sure I was going to slip and blurt it out. You know, say something like, 'Well, Brad, I guess I'll see you Thursday night at your surprise party.' How does Mike plan to get him over there?"

"He told Brad he's taking him into Ocean Beach to celebrate his birthday. They'll pass Jenny's house on the way and Mike will suddenly remember that he borrowed Scott's locker key at the club but forgot to return it. Then Mike will suggest that they stop in at Jenny's so she can give it to Scott in the morning."

"Sounds pretty complicated to me."

"I know. But I think Mike'll be able to pull it off."

"Let's hope so." I poured the batter into the pans, and Elizabeth stirred and spread it. Kim set the timer for thirty minutes as I slid them into the oven.

After we finished cleaning up, Kim and I sat down on the living room sofa and Elizabeth worked on her jigsaw puzzle. Within minutes the whole room smelled like chocolate. Kim picked up a copy of *Seventeen*. "I wish I could do something like this with my hair." She pointed to a beautiful picture on the cover. The model was wearing her hair in a long, thick braid.

"It's just a French braid. You could do that easily," I said. Kim's hair was light brown and very full. It fell way down below her shoulders.

"Are you kidding? I could never do that myself. I'm lucky I can comb my own hair."

"I'll do it for you if you like."

"You know how?"

"Sure. You could wear it like that to Jenny's party tonight. You'll look fantastic."

"What's a French braid?" I knew Elizabeth would be putting her two cents in before too long.

"It's a special kind of braid, Elizabeth. You divide your hair into lots of different sections."

"Can you fix my hair in a French braid? I'm sick of regular braids."

"Maybe."

"Good. Then I can look fantastic too."

The phone rang, but Elizabeth answered it before I could get there.

"Hello," she said. "Oh, hi, Brad. We were just baking brownies for your birth—"

"Elizabeth!" I shouted. I grabbed the receiver away from her, stopping her just in time. "Hi, Brad."

"Hi. What was that all about?"

"Oh, nothing. Just Elizabeth. You know how it is."

"Mike and I are going into Ocean Beach tonight for my birthday."

"Oh, that's right. I keep forgetting. It's your birthday." I looked at Kim and she started to crack up.

"I thought you might like to come along."

"Uh, sure." With Kim staring right at me, I had all I could do to keep myself from laughing.

"Great. We'll probably stop by and get Kim first, so I guess we'll be at your place around nine."

"See you then," I said and hung up. "He doesn't suspect a thing," I said to Kim. "He thinks he's coming over here on the way to Ocean Beach tonight. Oh, yeah, you're coming too." I chuckled. "They're picking you up first."

"That's too much. Hey, I think I just heard the timer."

The three of us ran into the kitchen.

"I don't know how they're going to taste, but they sure smell good," I said as I took the brownies out of the oven.

"You said I could have one, remember?" Elizabeth pleaded.

"Okay. One. They just have to cool a little."

Kim and I each took a pan and cut the brownies into little squares.

"Are they cool yet?" Elizabeth asked eagerly.

"Oh, I guess so. What do you say, Kim? Do you think we should test them?"

"Absolutely. We'd better make sure they're all right before we bring them to Jenny's."

"Good point."

"Mmmm," Kim said. We all agreed. "On a scale of one to ten," she added, "they're definitely a ten."

Before Kim went home, I did her hair in a French braid. She had to take a shower, change, and all that stuff, but she was coming back at about seven so we could go to Jenny's together. I didn't want to face Jenny alone. It was always a good idea to have Kim around for moral support.

I took Brad's birthday present out of my closet and put it on the bed so I wouldn't forget it. I had gotten him a record album in Ocean Beach. Maybe he'd think of me every time he played it. I hoped he'd play it a whole lot. I wrapped it in the funnies from the Sunday paper. I always saved the funnies for wrapping paper. I hate that stuff that says Happy Birthday all over it.

I wanted to look my best. I knew there would be lots of competition. Jenny and her friends always looked so perfect. I decided to wear my white designer jeans and a teal blue silk blouse. It was a very simple outfit, but I felt elegant in it. Besides, the blue blouse matched my eyes, and the white pants showed my tan.

I hoped that I would get a chance to really talk to Brad. There was so much that I didn't know about him. Ever since Kim had told me about his girl-friend, I had been dying to know more about wondered why Brad had never mentioned her. Yet again, I had never mentioned Randy. Did Brad feel as confused as I did? If I knew how he felt about us, it would have been a lot easier to figure out my own feelings. Kim had told me that I should ask him indirectly, but how would I go about it? Supposing he started talking about Catherine—did I want to tell him about Randy?

Oh, well, I thought, I probably won't get a chance to talk to Brad anyway. Jenny had invited about thirty people, mostly kids from Sea Gate. They all knew Brad well. I'd met some of them at the club but didn't exactly feel free and easy with them. Jenny had told me that some of the kids would be bringing beer, but I didn't like the idea too much. Kim wasn't into that either, so at least I wouldn't be the only one. I just hoped that we wouldn't look like a couple of nerds.

"Hi. Elizabeth let me in," said Kim, plopping onto my bed. "Wow! You look terrific. New jeans?"

"No. I just haven't worn them here before. You look good too."

Kim was wearing a little bit of blusher and some lip gloss. Very unusual for her.

"Thanks. I thought I'd try a little makeup to go with my new hairstyle. What do you think?" She held *Seventeen* up next to her face.

"I think you look every bit as pretty as the cover girl," I said truthfully.

"I wish. Hey, guess what? I got a letter from my father today. He loves London. He said he wishes he could stay there forever."

"It would be neat if you could visit him there."

"I doubt it. He'll be home at the end of the summer. By the way, how have things been with your folks?"

"Okay, I guess. Mom says everything's fine, but sometimes I still worry."

"Yeah, I know what you mean."

"I'll tell you, Kim, I don't know how you do it. If they ever got divorced I don't think I could handle it nearly as well as you have."

All of a sudden Schnapps started barking like crazy outside my room. Kim and I ran into the hall and practically tripped over Elizabeth crouched by the doorway.

"Elizabeth, you little nerd, what are you doing up here?" I screamed.

"Playing with Schnapps," she said.

"It isn't nice to eavesdrop on people. I don't listen when you talk to your dumb friends."

"I know, but . . ."

"But what?"

"I just wanted to hear what you guys were saying about Mom and Dad." She quickly brushed away a tear. "Is Dad going to go away again?"

"Of course not, Elizabeth. Dad loves us very much. He'd never leave us."

"Are you sure?"

"Positive."

"Well, then, what was all that stuff you and Kim were saying?"

"We were saying that everything's just fine." I guess it really was pretty rough on the kid, but she looked very much relieved. "I have an idea, Elizabeth. Why don't you come downstairs with Kim and me and we'll give you a supply of brownies."

"Really? Gee, thanks."

"Come on, Kim. If we don't hurry up, Brad will arrive at Jenny's before we do."

Instead of walking up the beach the way we usually did, Kim and I took Bay Walk into Sea Gate. We were wearing our good jeans and we didn't want to look as though we had been caught in the middle of a sand storm by the time we got to the party.

"You know where Jenny's house is, right?" Kim asked.

"I've never been there, but she told me it's at the end of Ocean View Terrace. She said you couldn't miss it."

We turned onto Jenny's street and walked toward the ocean. Jenny wasn't kidding. You sure couldn't miss her house. "That must be it," I said, pointing to a huge structure overlooking the beach. "Jenny said it was the only house on the street that was right on the ocean."

Kim and I had never seen anything like it. It looked like one of those houses you see in magazines like *House and Garden*. I didn't think anyone really lived in houses like that. It was ultramodern, with lots of patios and lots of different levels. There were big windows everywhere.

"Wow! Can you believe this? I think we'll need a map to find the front door," I said.

"Do you think they'll let us in?" Kim joked.

"Probably not, but let's try, anyway."

Jenny appeared in the doorway in a white off-the-shoulder sundress.

"Lauren, Kim, I'm so glad you could come," she said.

"Nice little place you've got here," Kim said as we went in the front door.

"Thanks. It's still a little rough," Jenny apologized. "Mother's been decorating for ages but it's not quite finished."

I admired the beautiful entry hall with its shiny wooden floor and high ceiling. The living room was elaborately furnished with glass tables and chintz print sofas and chairs. If it's still in the rough, I thought, I can't even begin to imagine what it'll look like when it's finished.

"Here, Jenny. We made some chocolate fudge brownies."

"Thanks. I'll put them in the kitchen. Why don't you go down to the lower level and join the others? I'll be there in a sec."

We took the big wooden staircase downstairs to a large family room. There were glass doors all around it that led out to a deck and to the beach. I looked around and, thank goodness, there were a few kids I at least recognized. Susan something or other, one of Jenny's girlfriends, was across the room talking to Cindy Olson. I liked Cindy. She was friendly and energetic. She was cute too—petite with long blond hair down to her waist and big green eyes—but she wasn't snobby or anything. There were a few other kids who looked familiar, but I didn't know their names. I figured Brad would introduce me later.

Jenny came downstairs. "Listen, everybody, Brad should be here any minute. I'll turn out most of the lights down here so he can't really see anything. And one more thing. Try to keep the noise down to a low roar so he'll be surprised."

"This is so exciting," I whispered to Kim.

"Yeah, I guess. I don't know a soul here, though."

"Don't worry about it. We'll fake it."

Oh, no. Scott was coming over.

"Hi. I'm Scott Harrington. Aren't you Lauren, Brad's partner in the tournament?"

"Yes. Nice to meet you." I wondered how he knew my name. "This is my friend Kim."

"Hi," Kim said. I could tell she was sizing him up.

"You know, Lauren, you're getting quite a reputation around the club," Scott said.

"Reputation? Me?"

"Rumor has it that you're something else on the courts. I know Jenny is worried."

Jenny's worried about *me?* "Oh, well, Brad and I have been working pretty hard, if that's what you mean."

"Lauren, don't be so modest," Kim chimed in. "Tell Scott about the time you beat Chris Evert in straight sets when you were down in Florida last year." She was so serious I almost believed her myself.

Scott looked uneasy. "What?" he cried. "You've played the *pro* circuit?"

"She's only kidding," I assured him.

"Quiet, everybody," Jenny called from the top of the stairs. "Brad and Mike are coming to the front door."

The room was suddenly silent. We could hear Brad, Mike, and Jenny upstairs.

"Brad, Mike, what are you doing here?" Jenny asked innocently.

"Hi, Jen," Mike said. "What are you all dressed up for?"

"Oh, Dad's taking us to the club for a late dinner."

"Listen," he continued, "I forgot to give Scott his locker key and I thought he might need it tomorrow."

"Thanks," Jenny said. "I'll give it to him in the morning. Brad," she went on, "I know we're on rival teams and everything, but I think my tennis racket is warping. Would you mind taking a quick look at it? It's right downstairs."

"Sure, Jen. I'd be happy to. Just leave it to Dr. Caldwell."

I gave Kim a disgusted look.

"Just follow me," Jenny instructed.

I could hardly wait to see Brad's face when he came down and saw everyone.

"Surprise!" we yelled.

Brad was absolutely stunned. He sat down on the steps in a state of shock. Everyone rushed over to him to wish him a happy birthday. There were so many people around him I couldn't get anywhere near him.

"I don't believe this," Brad kept saying. "How come nobody said anything?"

"Because it's a surprise party, you dummy," Mike said, laughing.

Brad finally saw me in the back, behind the other kids. We started to make our way toward each other.

"Happy birthday," I said, kissing him on the cheek. He kissed me right back. On the lips, though.

"I guess you knew about this all along."

"Yeah. It's been awful keeping it from you."

"I'm impressed. I could never keep a secret like that."

"Why do you think I've been avoiding you so much for the past couple of days?"

"Yeah, come to think of it, I did notice that you seemed to be busier than usual."

Someone turned on the stereo and a bunch of kids immediately got up to dance.

"May I have this dance?" Brad asked, kissing my hand like someone out of the eighteenth century.

"I'd be honored." I giggled.

We danced to a fast song and I was really surprised. Brad was a great dancer! Most guys are total klutzes. They either stand there and tap their feet a little or they freaked out all over the floor and you want to die! Not Brad. I guess it just came naturally to him.

The next song was slow. As we danced he ran his fingers through my hair. I wished the song would never end. I could see Jenny giving me the evil eye from across the room. She came over when the song was over.

"So, Brad, tell me the truth, were you surprised?" she asked.

"I'll say. It was really nice of you to do this for me, Jenny. This is the first time anyone has ever given me a surprise party."

"Oh, it was nothing, Brad. I had lots of help. Scott brought some beer and Timmy brought something to spike the punch. And Lauren even baked some brownies! Isn't she sweet? Wasn't it your grandmother's recipe or something, Lauren?"

I don't know if it was her tone of voice or what, but she managed to make my brownies sound like the stupidest thing in the world. My face was turning five different shades of red, and, worst of all, I couldn't even think of anything to say to her.

Brad came to the rescue. He turned to me and smiled. "How did you know that I love brownies?"

Jenny looked annoyed. "That reminds me." She sighed. "I have to check on a few things in the kitchen."

"So where are these famous brownies of yours, Lauren? I'm starved "

We went over to a table covered with a big birthday cake, cookies, and my good old brownies.

"You really made these?" Brad asked, taking a big bite.

"Yes, really."

"Fantastic. The best I ever had."

"Oh, you're just saying that."

"No, it's true. I know a great brownie when I taste one," he said with a smile. "How about some punch?"

I wondered if Timmy really had poured something into the punch or if Jenny was just making that up. I decided to play it safe. "Uh, no. Uh—I don't think so," I stammered.

"Is something the matter?"

"No, nothing at all. I'm just not very thirsty."

Brad poured a glass for himself and took a sip. "Pretty strong stuff, but not bad. Sure you don't want some?"

"No thanks. Not right now."

"It's okay, Lauren."

"What's okay?"

"I mean you don't have to make excuses."

"What do you mean?"

"Like that night when we went to Bay Shore and

you didn't want to go to the Rusty Nail. And now you won't want any punch. Nobody's forcing you, you know. If you don't want a drink, just say so."

"I guess I just don't like it." I didn't know what else to say.

"You don't have to explain anything. Just do what you want."

He seemed to understand how I felt but I couldn't be sure. What if he thought I was really immature? I didn't care what the other kids did. That didn't bother me. The only thing that really scared me was that if my parents ever found out that kids were drinking at this party, that would be the end of me and Brad.

"My parents would really flip out."

"I thought that might be it. How come you're so uptight about your parents? You were scared to death that night we missed the ferry too."

"You wouldn't understand." I had never told him my real age and I wasn't planning to. Especially at that moment.

"You're a big girl, Lauren, and you've got a good head on your shoulders. You should be able to take care of yourself."

"It isn't that, Brad." I hesitated, wondering whether or not I should go on. "Maybe someday I'll be able to explain."

"All right. I won't cross-examine you anymore." He smiled. "Why don't we go out to the deck? I want you to meet some of my friends."

He introduced me to a few of the guys he knew from prep school. They knew Catherine. In fact, they were probably comparing me to her, I thought.

"Who's that guy over there?" I pointed to a quiet looking kid standing alone in the corner of the deck.

"Oh, that's Chuck the Nerd. He went to prep school with me too."

"Chuck the Nerd?" I repeated. "That's terrible. He looks kind of quiet, but he seems like a nice kid."

"Oh, Chuck's a great guy. He's not really a nerd or anything. In fact, he's a real riot. We just call him that because he got the highest mark in our class on the college entrance exams."

"Wow. I'll be lucky if I barely pass."

Brad kept me so busy I hardly saw Kim all evening, but she seemed to be having a terrific time with Mike. The party got a little rowdy toward the end, but it was all in fun. No damage was done or anything. And, you know, I don't think the punch was really spiked because no one got drunk. A few of the guys, including Brad, did sneak a beer or two, but it was no big thing. And Brad was right. Chuck the Nerd sure wasn't a nerd. He turned out to be the life of the party. He brought a bunch of water pistols and started an all-out war on the deck. I've never had so much fun.

By eleven thirty quite a few kids had already left, and I think Brad could tell that I was getting a little wilted.

"Feel like walking home along the beach?" he whispered in my ear.

"Sounds nice."

Jenny came floating by with a bucket of ice.

"Hey, Jen, great party," Brad said. "Thanks for everything. I think we're going to split."

"So soon? That's a shame," Jenny said. "We haven't even danced yet, Brad. Come on, a slow

115

song's on. You don't mind, do you, Lauren?" She shoved the ice bucket into my arms and took Brad by the hand. The next thing I knew they were dancing. Slow. And very close. Brad didn't seem to mind one bit, either. I hoped that it was just for old times' sake.

When they returned, I tried to pretend that nothing was wrong. Actually I wanted to dump the ice bucket over Jenny's head. Instead I just casually handed it back to her and smiled politely.

"Thanks for the dance, Brad," Jenny said. "Oh, and don't forget to stop by tomorrow and pick up your presents."

"See ya, Jen," Brad said. "And thanks again."

We slipped out the glass doors and then went down the steps to the sand. It was a nice night and the beach was deserted. As soon as I was alone with Brad again everything was all right. I wouldn't have cared if it took forever to get home.

We were about halfway to my house when Brad stopped walking.

"Let's sit down for a minute," he said.

"Don't tell me you're tired."

He looked at me impishly. "Of course I'm not. Come here."

He spread out his windbreaker and we sat down. Then he wrapped his arms around me and kissed me for the longest time. We slowly fell back into the sand and he kissed me again and again. It felt so nice. I didn't want him to stop. But still, I knew we shouldn't be there alone together.

"Brad, no."

"What's the matter?"

"We shouldn't."

"We're not doing anything wrong. We're only kissing."

"I know, but . . ." I sat up and turned away from him.

"Lauren, sometimes I can't figure you out."

"It's late. I should be getting home."

He was staring out into the ocean, not saying anything.

"Please don't be mad," I said softly.

"I'm not. It's my own fault. Let's go."

We didn't say a whole lot the rest of the way home, but Brad did hold my hand. When we got to my door he kissed me good night, just like he always did.

"I hope you had a happy birthday."

"Thanks. Yeah, it wasn't bad. I guess I'll see you tomorrow at practice." He took a few steps and then turned around. "Hey, your brownies really were great."

We both started to laugh, and I waved to him as he walked off.

I went straight upstairs when I got inside. I was so tired I washed my face in about thirty seconds. I changed into the old Indiana University T-shirt that Ellen's older sister had given me and fell into bed. Maybe I should have told him about my parents. Then he'd understand why I was so uptight all the time.

I kept thinking about the walk home. He had said he wasn't mad but I could tell he was. Just a little. Well, maybe not mad, but hurt or something. What was I supposed to do? It just didn't seem right to be there with him all alone on the beach and kiss him like that. Not that I didn't enjoy it. But I just knew it would have gotten too intense. I really liked Brad, but I didn't want to get in over my head.

I turned out the light and closed my eyes. My horoscope kept haunting me. "A new romance may become complicated after the seventh," it had said. It was really uncanny.

9

I never thought the day would come. In exactly three hours and fifteen minutes the Sea Gate Beach Club Annual Tennis Tournament would be officially underway. I'd been a nervous wreck all morning. Everybody had been avoiding me. I couldn't blame them. I kept doing spaced-out things. When I was getting dressed, I almost sprayed Mom's hairspray under my arms. It was right next to my deodorant on the bathroom shelf. I just picked up the wrong can. Fortunately I stopped myself in the nick of time. That would have been a pretty sticky situation. After breakfast I put my empty tea cup in the refrigerator. But that was nothing. The best was yet to come. I had decided to take Schnapps for a walk and got all the way down to the end of Sandy Lane before I realized I had Schnapps' leash in my hand, but no

Schnapps. Pretty scary. Schnapps ran in the other direction when I came back inside the house.

All morning I'd been trying to follow Brad's advice. He'd said, "Just keep repeating our motto over and over again. 'Think Wimbledon.'" I was so petrified you'd think I really was playing in Wimbledon. I wondered if the real pros got scared before a big match. They were probably used to the tension and the excitement of the crowds in the grandstands. It was the first time I had played for a crowd. There wouldn't exactly be thousands of fans at the club, but I had noticed someone setting up the bleachers the day before. Brad had said that once we got going, this wouldn't bother me, but now it did. It decidedly did.

Brad and I had been practicing like mad the last couple of weeks. He'd helped me improve my game so much that I was willing to bet I would make the school tennis team in the fall. I had wanted to be on the team since freshmen year. I'd almost made it. I was cut in the final round. But as they say, almost isn't good enough. It's tougher when you come really close than when they cut you right away. I was disappointed for days. It was Randy who got me over it. He told me he had been cut from the swim team the first year he'd tried out. And by junior year he was co-captain. Randy said you just have to keep at it. I was keeping at it, all right, but I doubted in quite the way Randy had in mind.

I hadn't mentioned that much about the tournament in my letters to Randy. I didn't want him to suspect anything. I wished that Randy could somehow see me play in the tournament, without Brad in the picture, of course. I knew he'd be so proud of me. I could practically hear him cheering me on.

I looked up at the sky and noticed a gigantic black cloud moving in. It wouldn't dare rain on the first day of the tournament! Not after all our hard work. Please, please, blow over to the mainland, I begged.

"Hi," Kim said as she came around to the deck. "What's with these clouds?"

"I don't know. Can you believe this?"

"They'll probably go out to sea," Kim assured me. "That's what those weather people always say, anyway."

"I sure hope so. I just want to get this first match over with."

"I brought you sort of a present."

"Sort of a present?"

"Yeah. It's my lucky ring. My Aunt Cecilia brought it back from France a few years ago. I always wear it for big tests and I haven't flunked one yet. You can borrow it if you like."

"Thanks." The ring was gold, with a tiny ruby set in it. "Are you sure it's okay? This is really nice."

"Sure. It's lucky. Nothing will happen to it. Does it fit?"

"Perfectly." I admired the dainty ring on my finger.

"When you look at it during the tournament, just remember I'm out there rooting for you."

"Thanks, Kim. It'll help a lot."

"So are you all psyched up?" she asked eagerly.

"Terrified is the right word, I think."

"Come on, after all your practice you should be an old pro."

"Believe me, I'm working at it. This morning I was a regular basket case. I took the dog for a walk and forgot the dog."

"That's serious."

"I'm starting to feel a little better now."

"It's going to be a piece of cake," she said smoothly. "You'll be a smash. I'm sure of it."

"I wish I were half as sure as you are."

"No sweat. Believe me, you can't lose. Listen, I've got to go meet Mike. We'll see you later at the courts."

"I'll look for you guys."

After Kim left, I went upstairs to get dressed. The week before, I had bought a new tennis dress at Fifteen, Love, a cute tennis shop in Ocean Beach. I had decided it was worth it to splurge some of last year's baby-sitting money. Kim and I both agreed that if I had a nice dress and looked like a real pro, I'd have the psychological edge.

I carefully slipped it over my head and zipped up the back. I'd have to get Elizabeth to hook it later. I really felt good in it. Like I should be out there giving my all. But still, it didn't seem like this could really be happening to me. Here I was playing in my first tournament ever. That was enough excitement right there. But to have someone like Brad as my partner besides. It was almost unreal. A few months before I never would have dreamed that a guy like Brad would even talk to me. I really wanted to do well. At first I had thought winning wasn't important. But now it was. I didn't want to disappoint Brad. I wanted him to be proud of me.

I picked up Kim's ring and slid it onto my left ring

finger. I wondered if it would really bring me good luck. Well, it certainly couldn't hurt.

"How come you're wearing your hair to the side like that?" Elizabeth asked as she came bouncing into the room.

"I just wanted to try something different."

"Oh." She paused and looked at me. I couldn't tell whether or not she liked it. "Mary Beth Parsons wore her hair like that in our school play last year," she went on. "She was Pocahontas."

I wondered if I looked like Pocahontas. I wasn't sure I wanted to.

"Very interesting, Elizabeth. Do me a big favor and hook the back of my dress, okay?"

"Sure. Are you scared?" she asked as she reached up and fastened the hook.

"Why should I be scared?" I tried to control my trembling voice.

"I don't know. I'd be scared stiff. You know, you have to win the first match or you're out. Not to mention all those people watching. I wouldn't be able to play."

"Okay, okay. If you don't cut it out I really will be scared. I've got to get down to the courts. See you later."

"Don't do anything dumb if you can help it."

"Thanks, Elizabeth. You're a real inspiration."

I took off for the club. As I was walking, I ran through my checklist in my head. I didn't want to forget anything important. Not today. Racket, towel, Kim's ring, jeans and T-shirt for later. They'd supply the tennis balls.

Brad was meeting me at our usual table on the

patio at one o'clock. We thought we'd review our strategy and then watch some of the men's singles match. We weren't scheduled to play for another hour, and when I got to our table I found Brad casually leaning back in his chair reading *The Fire Island News*. He was as relaxed as could be. You'd never know he was about to play in a tennis tournament. He looked like a celebrity in his white tennis shorts and sunglasses. My heart started to beat a little faster when I sat down with him. He was so involved in the paper he didn't even see me.

"Excuse me, sir, but aren't you Brad Caldwell, the famous tennis star?"

"Ha, ha. How's my favorite mixed doubles partner?"

"Okay now. But this morning I was really out to lunch. I thought my parents were going to exile me to the mainland."

"Nothing to be nervous about. We're going to beat those turkeys easily. Steve Nash doesn't know a backhand from a touchdown pass, and Diane Lawson couldn't return a serve to save her life."

"Let's just hope they haven't suddenly improved."

"Not a chance. We'll just stick to our game plan. You play the net and I'll cover the back court. Nothing fancy, just good solid tennis."

"Got it."

A waiter came over with two glasses of orange juice.

"I ordered before you came. O.J.'s good for energy. By the way, that's a great tennis dress. And your hair looks terrific like that." He pushed his sunglasses up on top of his head and looked straight at me.

"Thanks."

He looked serious again. "Look, Lauren, when you're out there, I want you to pretend it's just another practice session. Concentrate extra hard. And don't forget, winning is a state of mind."

"I know. And think Wimbledon."

"Absolutely. How about it, champ? Ready to go check out the courts? The men's singles match should be underway."

"Love to."

Brad signed the check and we were on our way to the courts. We stood behind the fence watching the two men's singles contenders, Jeff Armstrong and Brian Reese. They were playing a hard set.

"They're looking pretty good, don't you think?" Brad commented.

"I'll say. They're really playing for blood. You know, Brad, I've been meaning to ask you this. How come you didn't enter the men's singles?"

"I don't know. I guess I just got tired of it."

"Tired of it?"

"Yeah, well, I've won the past two years."

I couldn't believe it. He'd actually won the men's singles title two years in a row. And he mentioned it so matter-of-factly.

"Why didn't you tell me?"

"I thought you knew. Besides," he added with a smile, "I think mixed doubles is much more interesting."

He leaned over and kissed me. I put my arms around his neck and kissed him back.

"No fair distracting your partner," he whispered. "We've got serious work to do, but I promise we'll make up for it later."

As we watched Jeff and Brian battle it out, I couldn't help noticing how intimidating the courts seemed. There were line judges, announcers, and ballboys and -girls, just like in a real tournament. The bleachers had to be the worst. Somehow I'd just have to get used to the idea of people watching me.

"This isn't so bad, is it?" Brad said confidently.

"Uh, no, I guess not." I hesitated. "It just seems so different with all these spectators here."

"What spectators?"

"You know. The people in the bleachers."

"What bleachers?"

"Brad, don't be silly. They're right over there. Plain as can be." He grinned at me and shook his head. When I finally realized what he was doing, I laughed. "Oh, I get it. Those people out there really aren't out there."

"That's right," he said with a smile. "They're just a figment of your imagination. Pretend they're not there and you'll play like you always do. It's easy."

Easy for him, maybe. He made it sound so simple. I wished I had half his self-confidence.

The loud cheering from the bleachers drew my attention back to the courts. The final point was scored. Jeff had won the preliminary round in the men's singles division and would continue to play in the competition. Brian looked awful. I couldn't tell if he was exhausted or just disappointed. That's the bad thing about a tournament. Somebody has to lose.

"Come on, Lauren. We should check in with the officials. We'll be starting soon."

My stomach felt as though it was going to fall out. We gave our names to the officials and then we sat down on the players' bench. Brad, of course, was completely cool.

I glanced up at the bleachers to see if I could spot Mom, Dad, and Elizabeth. Kim and Mike were supposed to be out there somewhere too. They all looked like a big blur. Didn't those people have anything better to do than watch amateur tennis? Maybe if I yelled "FIRE!" they'd all leave. From the corner of my eye I noticed a head bobbing up and down in the second row. It was Elizabeth. She was waving her arms desperately, trying to catch my attention. She looked pretty funny, but I was glad I'd found her. Mom, Dad, Kim, and Mike were sitting with her, and they were waving madly now too. I felt a lot better knowing they were out there.

As I waved back, I heard the voice come over the loudspeaker.

"Ladies and gentlemen, the preliminary round of the mixed doubles competition is about to begin on court seven."

Brad squeezed my hand. There was a lump in my throat at least the size of a golf ball.

The announcer continued. "Miss Diane Lawson and Mr. Steve Nash will play Miss Lauren McDermott and Mr. Brad Caldwell. Please welcome them."

There was a round of applause as we made our way out to the court. I took my place in front of the net and Brad was behind me. My legs were trembling. That wasn't the worst of it. My palms were all sweaty too. What if my racket slipped out of my hand? I glanced down at Kim's lucky ring. Please help me get through this, I wished. Brad came up behind me and said softly, "Remember, *think Wimbledon.*"

Before I had a chance to get any more terrified, Steve served the first ball and Brad returned it. There was no turning back now. We were finally into it. Brad was right again. Once we started playing, the people in the bleachers didn't even enter my mind. Every ounce of concentration was focused on my shots. Nothing else existed except me, Brad, Diane, Steve, and the tennis court.

We were playing a standard three-set match. Whoever won two out of three sets would win the match. I have to say that the first few games of the first set were a nightmare. If it hadn't been for Brad we would have lost for sure. Toward the end of the first set I started to play a little better, but it was mostly because of Brad's hard work that we won it, six games to two.

The second set was even tougher. I was playing pretty well, but, unfortunately, so were Diane and Steve. I finally felt a little bit at ease. The score was tied at two games all. The next thing I knew, they had crept up on us. We were losing the set two to four. Somehow I managed to return some difficult serves and hit an impossible backhand volley. Luck must have been with us. We were able to tie it up at four all. From that point on Brad and I rallied. We even broke service to finally win the second set, six to four. It was Brad who made the final shot with a tricky lob. I nearly passed out when I heard the announcer say, "Game, set, and match to Miss McDermott and Mr. Caldwell."

Brad and I ran to the net to shake hands with Diane and Steve. After we'd all thanked each other and finished with the formalities, it finally hit us. *We did it. The two of us.* We had actually won the preliminary round and now we were on our way!

The next thing I knew, lots of people had gathered around us on the court. Brad's parents, his little brother, Billy, my parents, and Elizabeth. It was a wonderful feeling.

In the middle of all the hubbub I felt Elizabeth tapping me on the shoulder. "Who's that kid with the baseball glove?" she asked, pointing to Brad's brother.

"That's Brad's little brother, Billy. He's ten."

"Oh, yeah. I guess he kind of looks like Brad. The blond hair and all."

"Elizabeth, I thought you weren't interested in boys."

"I'm not. I was just wondering who would be dumb enough to bring a baseball glove to a tennis match."

"Come on, I'll introduce you."

"No. That's okay."

I took her by the hand and practically dragged her over.

"Billy, I'd like you to meet my sister, Elizabeth. Elizabeth, this is Brad's brother, Billy."

"Hi," Billy said.

"Hi," Elizabeth mumbled.

They looked up, down, and everywhere but at each other as they stood there fidgeting.

"What grade are you in?" Billy finally managed.

"Fifth. How about you?"

"Sixth."

"How come you brought a baseball glove to a tennis match?" Elizabeth asked bluntly.

"Oh, I'm in the Fire Island Little League. I've got to play in a big game tonight," Billy boasted. He sounded just like his brother.

We left Billy and Elizabeth and walked over to the end of the patio where we could look out over the ocean. It was about four thirty, and there were hardly any people left on the beach. Just a couple of die-hard sun worshippers. This time of day was my favorite. It was always so nice and quiet. The busy daytime activities were over and the nightlife hadn't yet begun.

"I thought you did great out there today, Lauren." Brad's hair was blowing in the breeze as he leaned against the patio railing.

"Thanks. You were pretty good yourself."

"I knew we'd be able to do it. From now on, we just have to keep on playing like we did today and everything'll be fine."

"I hope you're right. I'm just glad the first match is over."

"I know how you feel. I remember how it was for me in my first tournament. My knees were so wobbly I almost couldn't stand up. The first is always the worst. But don't worry. In a day or so, when it really hits you, you'll be psyched up beyond belief to play the next match. And then the championship round will be here before we know it."

"That reminds me. My best friend from home will be here for the end of the tournament. She's coming

130

next week. I'm glad she could make it before the end of the season."

"It's incredible when you think about it. Summer's more than half over already."

"It's awful."

"I guess I'm kind of looking forward to college, but summer's always been my favorite time of the year. I'm going to miss you, Lauren."

"I'll miss you too."

"Oh, I'm sure you have lots of boyfriends back home in Garden City."

"Uh, no. Not really."

"Maybe one special one then?"

"How about you? Do you have a girlfriend?" I held my breath in anticipation. He couldn't possibly know that Kim already told me about Catherine.

"I've been seeing this girl on and off, but we're not serious or anything. She was just someone to go out with while I was in high school. We had a good time."

From what Kim had said, it didn't sound quite so casual. I wondered if he'd ever describe me as "just someone to go out with while he was on Fire Island."

"What about you?" he went on. "You never answered my question. Do you have a boyfriend or don't you?"

"I guess I sort of have one."

"That's what I figured. A girl as pretty as you doesn't sit around on Saturday night. I kind of wish I was going to be around so I could see you next year, but that's the way it goes, I guess. Hey, who knows? Maybe you'll come down to Princeton to visit me sometime."

"That sounds fun." I tried to sound cool but I was really excited. He wanted me to visit him! I would be the envy of every girl in school if I went to Princeton for the weekend! That is, if my parents allowed me to go. I couldn't imagine how I would ever convince them. If they thought Bay Shore was a big deal, wait until I dropped this one! I was happy that he wanted to see me even after the summer was over.

Suddenly we heard someone running toward us and we both turned around. It was Billy.

"Mike told me to find you and tell you this right away," he panted.

"What is it, Billy?" Brad asked.

"Jenny and Scott won their first match too. It just ended."

"Oh. Thanks a lot," Brad replied.

"See ya later." Billy dashed off.

"I just have this funny feeling that we're going to play them in the finals and it's going to be rough. Possible, but rough." Brad sounded very serious.

"Hey, coach. It'll be a piece of cake. Remember?"

"Right. You know, I think we left some unfinished business before," Brad said softly.

"Unfinished business?"

I was in his arms again and he was kissing me tenderly. He unfastened my hair ribbon with one gentle tug, and as my hair fell loosely around my shoulders he embraced me again and kissed me like I'd never been kissed before. I ran my fingers along his shoulders and down his arms, tracing the outline of his firm muscles. He kissed my lips, my cheeks, and even my hair. If the wind had picked us up and carried us out to sea, I wouldn't have cared. All of a sudden he lifted his head and looked deep into my eyes.

"I don't want this summer to ever end, Lauren," he said, cradling my head in his hands.

"Me either," I whispered. I barely got the words out, but it didn't matter. We both knew that something magical was happening.

10

I could hardly believe it, but we did it. Brad and I actually made it to the finals! We got through the quarters and the semis without much trouble at all. Except for the time in the semis when I served to the wrong side of the court and we lost the point. Very embarrassing. It didn't make any difference, though. We won the match anyway. And just as Brad had predicted, Jenny and Scott won in their division, too, so we'd be playing them for the title. It was sure to be one tough match.

Mom was making coffee when I went down to breakfast. I had to hurry up and eat. Ellen was arriving on the nine o'clock ferry. What a day!

"Good morning, Lauren. I guess today's the big day of the finals, isn't it?" Mom said brightly.

"Yeah. As Brad says, 'This is it. Do or die.' With his coaching I'm sure we'll do okay."

"Brad's quite an accomplished tennis player."

"He sure is. You know what? He won the men's singles title at the club last year and the year before. He's practically guaranteed a place on the Princeton team next year too." I took a deep breath. I figured this was as good a time as any. "Mom, Brad said he wanted me to visit him at school."

"At Princeton? You mean for a weekend?"

"Yeah, I think so."

"I'm sorry, Lauren, but I'm afraid that would be out of the question."

"Oh, come on, Mom. You know Brad. He's a great guy."

"The answer is no, Lauren. You're just too young for that sort of thing."

"But I'm seventeen. I'm not a baby. I'll probably be going away to school myself in another year."

"That's not the same thing. And if I were you I wouldn't even mention it to your father."

I guess that was a subtle hint. It just didn't seem fair. Parents sure can ruin everything for you. "What do you have against Brad, anyway?" I asked angrily.

"I think he's a nice boy, Lauren. He's just a little too . . ."

"Too what?"

"It's probably just that he's older, but sometimes he seems a little too fast compared to your other friends."

"What do you mean? Why do we have to compare him to my other friends?"

"Well, for one thing, Dad was at the club the other night with John Addison, and Brad was sitting at the bar with a friend drinking a beer."

"So what? He's eighteen."

"That's just what I mean, dear. And you're not. You'll do all those things in time."

"I never get to have any fun." I sulked.

Dad walked into the kitchen and kissed me on the cheek.

"How's our tennis star today?"

"Okay, I guess."

"Why the long face? You'd better perk up if you plan to clinch that mixed doubles championship," Dad advised.

"Don't worry. I will." I gulped down the rest of my orange juice and got up from the table. "I have to meet Ellen's ferry. See you guys later."

I bolted out the side door and headed for the ferry slip. Wouldn't you know it, I thought. An adorable hunk like Brad Caldwell invites me to Princeton and my mother won't let me go! You'd think I was a little kid! How would I ever tell Brad? Well, at least Ellen was coming. I would be able to talk to her. She would probably have some good suggestions.

There were a few other people waiting to meet the ferry. Of course, the usual little kids with wagons were hanging around the dock. They probably made a ton of money helping people carry their luggage.

As soon as the ferry started to pull in, I spotted Ellen. Who could miss her? By the end of the summer her blond hair was almost pure white. Good old El was taking full advantage of the beautiful sunshine on the deck. Her eyes were closed and she was leaning back against the captain's cabin.

"Hey, El," I called. "Over here."

She smiled and waved furiously when she saw me.

She must have run all the way down to the lower deck, because she was one of the first people off the boat.

"It's been ages," I said as we hugged each other. "How's everything back home?"

"Just great. Here, before I forget, Randy sent you this." She handed me a letter and I stuffed it in my hip pocket.

"I'll read it later. Right now we've got a lot to catch up on."

"So this is the famous Fire Island," she said as we turned up Bay Walk. "Not bad, not bad at all."

"It's been a terrific summer, El. I wish you could have been here the whole time. And I'm absolutely dying for you to meet Brad."

"He's the guy you've been playing tennis with, right?"

"Right. You'll meet him this afternoon at the tournament."

"From what you've said, he sounds pretty neat." She paused for a minute and then gave me a sidelong glance. "You know, Lauren, Randy really misses you. He looks completely lost without you."

"I miss him too."

"Boy, from all you've said about that Brad guy in your letters, I was beginning to think you didn't like Randy anymore."

"El, don't be silly. Randy's my boyfriend."

"You really had me worried there for a while."

"I guess Brad's sort of a boyfriend, too, but it's different."

"What are you going to do when the summer's over?"

"That's the big problem. I really want to go out

with Randy when I get home, but I don't want to lose Brad either."

"Sounds like you're playing with fire, Lauren. It's pretty hard to go out with two guys at the same time. I know I could never pull it off."

"I don't think I'll have to. It looks like my parents aren't going to let me visit Brad at Princeton."

"Hmmm. Mine probably wouldn't let me do that either."

"I'm afraid if I press the issue it'll cause a big scene, if you get my drift."

"I thought you'd stopped worrying about that stuff months ago."

"You know how I am."

"Well, how have things been?"

"All right." I kicked a big sea shell out of my path as I turned down Sandy Lane. "I just wish I could be sure they'd stay together forever."

"Look, if they're still together after all they've been through, their relationship's probably more solid than most."

"You sound just like Kim."

"Who?"

"My friend here on the island. You'll meet her later. She's terrific."

When we got to A Summer Place, we walked around back and went through the kitchen door. No one was around. They were probably down at the beach.

"Come on upstairs and you can dump your stuff. You'll be staying in my room."

We both slumped onto the beds and kicked off our sandals as soon as we got upstairs. I think El and I have spent half our lives sitting around in each

138

other's room talking for hours on end. It was so great to see her again.

"So what does Randy have to say?" she asked, reminding me of his letter.

"Oh, wow. I nearly forgot." I reached into my pocket and pulled out the letter. It was a little crumpled, but readable just the same. I skimmed it quickly.

Dear Laur,

I'm scribbling this to you in two seconds so I can drop it off at Ellen's before she leaves. Sorry if it's kind of a mess.

I got a couple of days off at the end of August and I'd really like to come out on the 30th. That's a week before Labor Day. I'll take the first ferry over and the last ferry back so we can have the whole day together. Can't wait to see you. Let me know if it's okay. Okay?

Love,
Randy

"He wants to come visit me."

"Lauren, that's great!" Ellen shrieked.

"Right."

"Is something wrong? I thought you said you still really like him."

"Oh, I do, El. More than ever. But how am I going to keep Brad out of the picture?"

"Simple. Just tell him you're busy. As a matter of fact, be straight with him. Tell him your boyfriend from home's coming to visit. Don't worry. He'll be cool about it."

"Do you really think so?"

"Sure. Look at it from Brad's point of view. The last thing he wants to do is run into your boyfriend. I mean, for all he knows, Randy could be a six-foot-six linebacker with a nickname like Moose or something."

"Moose?" I laughed hysterically. "You kill me, Ellen." But maybe she had the right idea. I'd just tell Brad the truth.

Ellen and I spent the better part of the morning gossiping and reminiscing. She filled me in on a whole bunch of stuff that was happening at home. Barbara and John had broken up. Debbie Collins was moving to Louisiana before Labor Day, so I probably wouldn't see her before she left. I promised myself I'd write to her. That conceited jerk Bob Morgan got a gorgeous 1970 Mustang convertible. In mint condition, of course. Now he'd really think he was the living end. I asked Ellen about that party Joni Hartman had. She said Randy hadn't brought anyone. He just sort of kept to himself most of the night and left about ten.

Kim came over after lunch and we all walked to the club together for the finals. After the quarters and the semis, I'd pretty much gotten used to the idea of playing in a tournament, so I wasn't really that nervous. Maybe just a little jumpy, but nothing like that first game. I'll say one thing, though. It sure was great having two good friends with me.

By the time we got to court seven, Brad was already warming up.

"There he is," I whispered to Ellen, setting my things on the bench.

"He certainly doesn't look too bad from here," Ellen said approvingly.

"You have to give Brad that much," Kim admitted. "He's a great looking package."

I wondered what she meant by that. "Shhh. He's coming over."

"You must be Ellen," Brad said, smiling brightly. He shook her hand, pouring on the old Caldwell charm full blast. "Lauren's told me all about you. It's a pleasure to meet you."

If I didn't know better I'd have sworn Ellen was blushing. "Oh, thanks. Lauren's said a lot about you too."

Thanks, El. Now he's going to think I talk about him all the time.

"How long are you staying?" Brad asked, securing his racket back into the press.

"Oh, just today and tomorrow."

"We'll have to show you the sights," Brad went on. "There's the beach, of course, the Sunken Forest, and we even have our own haunted house."

"Thanks. I'd love it. Wait a minute—haunted house?"

"Don't worry. It isn't really scary," Kim assured her.

It was almost game time and people were slowly drifting over to the bleachers.

"Come on, Ellen. Let's go find some good seats. Good luck, you guys," Kim continued. "Just think, next time we talk to you you'll be champs."

"Hopefully," I added.

"Definitely," Brad insisted. He looked at me and frowned. He hated it when I didn't think positive.

"Break a leg," Ellen called, blowing a kiss.

I winced. "Please, El. Don't say that! I just might!"

141

"Oops. Sorry. Just get out there and kill 'em."

"Nice kid. I can see why you're such good friends," Brad commented.

"Yeah. We've known each other forever."

"By the way, have you seen our good friends Jenny and Scott?" He squinted into the sun to try to find them.

"No, as a matter of fact I haven't. Maybe they chickened out."

"No such luck. They're probably plotting their attack, but it won't do them any good."

"Yesterday I took a couple of extra hours and practiced returning balls to an imaginary Jenny. Poor Jenny. She's going to be hitting backhands from me all afternoon."

"Right into the net, I hope." Brad laughed. "Speak of the devils! There they are now."

I watched them walk onto the court. Actually, Jenny and Scott didn't just walk. Jenny sort of bounced and Scott strutted.

"Well, this is it. The final showdown," Jenny said gaily as she passed.

"I hope you're ready for us, Jen," Brad said smugly. "It's not going to be easy."

"Are you kidding, Caldwell?" she shot back. "Scott and I are going to show you how the game is really played. Right, Scott?"

"Yeah, right. We plan to win every set."

"I wouldn't bet on it," Brad said confidently.

Jenny's eyes narrowed; I felt pretty uncomfortable.

"Well," I said to Jenny cheerfully, "break a leg!"

She just stared at me as Brad chuckled softly.

Each minute seemed to take an hour as we waited

for the match to start. I fumbled with the ribbon in my hair and straightened the strings on my racket. The bleachers were filled, the line judges were at their posts, and then, finally, the announcer made the introduction. At long last we were getting underway!

At first everything seemed to be going just great. Brad and I had our teamwork coordinated perfectly. But Scott hit some good shots and we lost the first game. I don't know how, but we lost the second game too. I was beginning to get nervous. Brad told me to keep cool. The match was far from over. We did manage to win three games, but we ended up losing the first set, six games to three.

Whoever won two sets would win the match, just like in the earlier rounds. So if we wanted to prevent Scott and Jenny from winning the match right off, we had to win the second set no matter what. The pressure was really on. The tension was stiffening the muscles in my neck and I could feel the perspiration dripping down my forehead. Brad and I were giving it two hundred percent.

I did all I could to hit to Jenny's backhand and it worked to our advantage. Whenever she hit a backhand, she'd send the ball straight into the net or out of bounds. Brad was slamming his killer serve across the court with all his might. It was practically unreturnable. Our strategy was working. We were ahead, four games to two.

Scott was really beginning to make me sick showing off. He was running all over the court to make the easiest shots look incredibly difficult. Athletes call it hot-dogging. He even asked one of the line judges to keep the spectators quiet so he could concentrate. What a nerd. Despite Scott's antics, we won the second set, thank goodness, six to three. Now we'd each won a set, and the championship would be decided by the third one.

Before the third set started, we took a short break. The players and officials congregated on the sidelines to rest and freshen up. Brad and I grabbed some cold water, Jenny tied her shoelaces, and Scott towel-dried his hair. I just quietly sat on the bench and tried to figure out how we were going to run Scott and Jenny right off the court.

"Hey, Scott," Brad teased, "how about a little mustard on that hot dog?"

"Very funny, Caldwell," Scott shot back. "You won't be laughing when we start dancing on you guys out there."

"We'll see about that, Harrington."

Brad glanced over at me and winked. I looked down at Kim's ring and nervously twisted it around. If it was ever going to bring me luck, I needed it now more than ever. I just knew we could do it. We were certainly the better team. Well, I thought so, anyway. We'd been practicing our sneakers off all summer long.

When we got back on the court for the third set, we got off on the wrong foot. About halfway through the first game the line judge ruled one of Brad's serves out of bounds, and he said Brad had stepped on the line to boot. Brad nearly blew a fuse. I'd never seen him short-circuit like that before. He started arguing with the judge, insisting the ball was in.

"Out?" Brad ranted. "What do you mean it was

out? It was clearly inside the line. Anyone could see that. You guys must need glasses or something." The judge glared. I wanted to disappear. I was sure they were going to kick us out of the tournament. Or maybe even off the island.

"I'm afraid we'll have to disqualify you from the match if this continues, Mr. Caldwell," the line judge said coldly.

Brad finally calmed down, but by then we were almost goners anyway. We lost that game and then we lost one more. Things just weren't going our way. The score was zero to two in games, Jenny and Scott's favor. I thought it was all over. They only needed four more games to win the set and match. The championship was slipping away.

The turning point came when I dropped my racket. The racket just flew out of my hands after a fairly easy forehand. My worst fear had come true. I couldn't have looked like a bigger clod if I'd tried. And all those people were watching! Somehow I managed to pick it up and then I did the most amazing thing. I came right back and hit a terribly difficult backhand that landed right in the back corner of Jenny and Scott's court. There was no way they could get to it. It looked like I'd planned to position it that way, but believe me, it was pure luck. I couldn't believe my eyes. The crowd broke into cheers, and when I glanced back at Brad he was beaming.

From that point on, Brad and I played as we'd never played before. We won six games in a row. When Brad scored the final point with a perfect dropshot, I wanted to toss my racket into the air and scream, "We did it!" We'd won the third set, six to two, and we'd won the match. Not only that, we won the championship.

Once again, just like in the prelims, the quarters, and the semis, we heard those wonderful words coming from the announcer: "Game, set, and match to Miss McDermott and Mr. Caldwell, the new Sea Gate Beach Club mixed doubles champions."

Brad ran into center court and leaped over the net to shake hands with Scott. Talk about hot dogs! I've only seen the pros do that on TV. I shook Jenny's hand, too, but not quite so enthusiastically.

"Congratulations," Jenny said bravely.

"Thanks. You sure gave us a good match." I was so out of breath I could hardly speak.

"Well, Lauren, we did our best. But I have to admit, you guys really outplayed us. I guess the best team won."

For a minute there I almost liked her, but I was on my guard. She leaned against the net and went on. "Maybe you could give me some pointers on my backhand sometime."

I stared at her in amazement. "Sure, Jenny. Anytime." I was completely baffled. Maybe she really was a decent kid underneath it all. Mom always said that snobbishness was usually a cover-up for insecurity, or something like that.

We suddenly became aware of the pandemonium around us. Players, officials, and spectators were being ushered into the clubhouse for a reception.

"I guess you'd better go enjoy the fanfare," Jenny said, nodding in the direction of the crowd.

"Yeah. I guess. Thanks again for a good match." I

picked up my racket and turned toward the club-house.

"Hey, Lauren," she called in her old taunting tone. "Next year Scott and I are really going to put up a fight, so you'd better be prepared."

"Don't worry, Jen," I said. "We'll be ready for you."

She gave me a genuine smile as I headed off. I still couldn't believe she wasn't up to something, but I decided to give her the benefit of the doubt. Between Jenny, the match, and all the excitement, I was in such a daze that I nearly bumped square into Brad on the way inside.

"What's with you? You look weird," he commented, studying the blank expression on my face.

"Oh, nothing. I've just been talking to Jenny."

"Well, forget about Jenny. I want to talk to you. Let's duck into the pro shop for a couple of minutes."

"Sure."

We made our way to the back of the shop where all the sports equipment was displayed.

"I just want to say thanks," he said.

"Thanks?" I asked.

"Yeah. For being such a terrific partner. I couldn't have done it without you."

I wanted to tell him that I was the one who should be thanking *him*. After all, if it hadn't been for Brad, I never would have gotten past the prelims. But, as usual, the words weren't coming out of my mouth. Luckily I didn't have to bother saying anything, because he put his arms around me and kissed me, right there in the middle of all the baseball bats and tennis rackets.

"I can think of things I'd rather do," he whispered, gently kissing my cheek, "but I guess we should join the party. We're supposed to be the guests of honor."

As soon as Brad and I entered the reception room, we were each presented with a beautiful silver trophy. I don't think I'd ever received a real trophy before. I promised myself I'd find a very special place for it at home.

Then *The Fire Island News* took our picture. I wished they had waited until after I had taken a shower and put some makeup on. After running around for two hours, I was kind of a wreck. To make matters worse, Elizabeth was standing behind the photographer making faces at me the whole time.

After we finished with pictures my parents and Kim and Ellen came rushing over.

"Sensational," Kim gasped.

"Your ring must have done the trick, Kim."

"Really, Lauren, where'd you learn to play like that?" Ellen shrieked. "I won't stand a chance on the courts with you anymore. You must be ecstatic."

"Are you kidding? I'm in a complete state of shock."

"I thought for sure you were going to blow it when you dropped your racket," Elizabeth said slyly. "I figured that was the end. I don't know how you ever pulled it out."

"Thanks, Elizabeth, for the support. You always did have faith in me."

Mom and Dad both kissed me. They were absolutely bubbling. I couldn't remember the last time I'd seen them so happy and proud.

Brad had a crowd of people around him too. The excitement calmed down a little when the refreshments were brought out, but that was only temporary. Brad got a beer for himself and an iced tea for me. I knew Mom would be less than impressed. When I turned around, I noticed her disapproving frown. Now it would be even more difficult to convince her that Brad wasn't, as she put it, "fast."

All I wanted to do was to be alone with Brad, but I knew that was impossible. I couldn't get within ten feet of him. There must have been twenty people hovering over him. He seemed to be enjoying all the attention. He was posing for photographs, greeting old friends, talking with club members. Some people are just born stars. I knew I'd see him tomorrow, so I didn't really mind that much.

I left toward the end of the party with my crew. They were a pretty loyal bunch. It was like having my own fan club, but nothing like Brad's. I was disappointed that I couldn't bring my trophy home, but it had to go to the engraver. They promised me I'd have it the following week.

After all the excitement it was great to come home to A Summer Place. Kim had to go back to her house to get ready for a date with Mike, so it was just Ellen and me. We lounged around in the living room watching some dumb old movie until it was time for dinner. When we sat down to eat, I noticed that someone had taped a sign to my chair. It said "The Champ" in big red, white, and blue letters. Very cute. It was probably Dad, but no one would admit to it.

After dinner El and I walked over to the bay to watch the sun set. It was a funny thing with El and me. No matter how much we talked, there was always more to say. And sometimes it was nice just to say nothing at all and enjoy each other's company. It was almost as if we each knew what the other was thinking.

As I stared into the sunset I couldn't get Randy out of my head. He was out there somewhere, right across the bay, but he might as well have been on the other side of the world. I kept wondering about his visit. I still wasn't quite sure I'd be able to swing it, but I knew there had to be a way. I just hadn't worked out all the details yet. Why did life have to be so complicated?

I was exhausted from the tournament and Ellen was tired from her trip, so we left the dock early and went home to hit the sack. Elizabeth nobly volunteered to camp out in the living room so Ellen could have her bed. I'd probably have to repay the favor at least a hundred times. I knew she'd never let me forget it. One time last spring I had to get to Randy's swim meet but my bike had a flat tire. Elizabeth lent me hers, but I think I dried the dinner dishes for her till August.

I was lying awake in bed thinking about the whole crazy day. I called across the room to Ellen. "Hey, El. You asleep?"

"Nope. I've been listening to the surf."

"It's nice, isn't it? I used to listen to it when we first got here. I think I've kind of gotten used to it now. It's like a lullaby." I closed my eyes and listened to the rhythm of the waves rolling in. "So tell me, what did you think of Brad?"

"Like you said, he's really cute."

"Well, did you think he was nice?"

"I guess. It's sort of hard to tell. I didn't have much time to talk with him. Did you let him know Randy's coming?"

"No. With all the excitement of the tournament I must have forgotten all about it."

"If I were you I'd tell him right away. Get it over with."

"Maybe tomorrow." I don't know why but I was getting the impression that Ellen didn't think too much of Brad. "You know," I added, "I don't think Kim likes Brad very much."

"No? Why not?"

"She thinks he's . . . I don't know . . . too cool or something."

"You're the one who has to like him. What do you think?"

"I don't know. He can't help it if he's a hunk and really terrific. Tomorrow you'll get to spend more time with him, so you'll see what he's really like."

"Great. Hey, don't forget to write to Randy tomorrow. I'll bring the letter back with me. He's dying to know if he can visit you."

"Okay. First thing."

"Good night."

"Night."

The next morning I was the last one down to breakfast. Everyone was standing around the table making a big fuss over *The Fire Island News.*

"Hey, Lauren, guess what?" Elizabeth screeched.

"Your picture's on the front page. Can I have your autograph?"

"Let me see that." Ellen handed me the paper and, sure enough, there we were. Brad looked fantastic, as usual. You'd never know he'd just played a whole tennis match. I had my eyes half closed and my hair was a disaster, but other than that I looked fine. The story wasn't too bad except for the part that told all about how Brad nearly got kicked out. I hated it when he did stuff like that. It was almost as dumb as the time he read the ferry schedule wrong and we almost got stuck in Bay Shore.

"Hi, everybody," Kim called through the screen door. "You guys ready to leave for Sea Gate?"

"I just have to get my towel. I'll be down in a minute." I ran upstairs to get my stuff together. By the time I came back down, everyone had cleared out of the kitchen. It was pretty quiet, but I could hear Ellen and Kim talking out on the deck.

"Lauren's really falling head over heels for him," I heard Kim say. I stepped back behind the kitchen door where they wouldn't be able to see me.

"Do you like him?" Ellen asked.

"Not really, but I don't want to hurt Lauren's feelings. He thinks he's really hot stuff. You know what I mean?" Kim went on.

"Yeah. It's too bad. And Randy's such a doll."

"What do you think Lauren's going to do, El?"

"Well, Randy's coming to visit soon, so maybe things will get back to normal once she sees him again."

"I hope so. Get this," Kim continued. "Mike says

he thinks Brad may just be using Lauren to get back at Jenny or something dumb like that."

"To get back at Jenny? Why?"

"Brad and Jenny used to be a major item two summers ago, but they had a big fight and broke up. That's why Brad was so intent on beating her in the tournament."

"You're kidding. That's pretty low."

"Well, I don't know if Brad's quite that low. I mean, he's probably not doing it deliberately. But still, I don't completely trust him. Let's face it, I just can't imagine a guy like Brad sitting around waiting for some girl in Garden City while he's off at college. Besides, he has another girlfriend at home named Catherine. Listen, El, don't breathe a word of this to Lauren. I don't want her to get hurt."

"Don't worry. My lips are sealed. We better keep it down," Ellen whispered. "She should be coming out any minute."

I felt as though someone had just dropped a bomb on my head, but I casually strolled out to the deck, trying to pretend I hadn't heard a thing.

"Ready to go, Lauren?" Kim asked, jumping up out of her chair as soon as she saw me.

"Sure."

"I'm dying to see this haunted house. Is Brad really going to take us over there?" El asked eagerly.

"I'm sure he'd love to."

I was angry at both of them. How could they say those things about Brad? Maybe they were just jealous. I tried to put it out of my mind as the three of us headed for Sea Gate.

On the way we ran into Brad on the beach. He was playing Frisbee with his little brother, Billy.

"Are you guys all set for the haunted house?" Brad asked.

"As ready as we'll ever be," Kim said.

"Well then, let's not waste any time. Follow me!"

We walked a little bit beyond the club and then up some steps that were built into the dunes.

"There it is. The old McGuire place. They say old man McGuire was a sea captain lost in a storm," Brad explained to Ellen.

Kim and I knew the whole story backward and forward. The house has been deserted for years, but people still claimed to hear strange sounds coming from inside. Every once and a while someone claimed to have seen a candle in an upstairs window or a pile of firewood on the front porch.

We walked toward the house rather timidly. It was pretty scary. I knew it was a crazy thought, but what if it really was haunted? I could just see the head-lines in *The Fire Island News*. FOUR TEENAGERS SWEPT AWAY BY UNKNOWN FORCE AT OLD MCGUIRE PLACE. MIXED DOUBLES CHAMPS ARE AMONG THE MISSING!

The house looked completely empty. It needed a coat of paint and a few new windows. The front yard could have used a little work too. We almost needed a machete to cut through the wild brush.

"Hey, look," Brad called. "You can see inside this front window."

"Any ghosts?" Kim asked sarcastically.

As Brad stepped away from the window he backed up into a rusty old garbage can, noisily knocking it to the ground.

"Oh, Caldwell. You're such a klutz. How'd you ever win a tennis tournament?" I kidded.

"What's going on out there!" a gruff voice shouted.

We all froze.

An old man appeared at the door. I was so frightened I didn't move a muscle. I couldn't really see the man's face, but he seemed to be smoking a pipe and wearing a hat.

"This is private property," the man snapped.

Something about him seemed vaguely familiar, but I just couldn't put my finger on it. Besides, he was standing in the shadow of the doorway.

Brad spoke up right away. "Sorry, sir. We were just passing through to the bay side."

"Next time take the regular path," he grumbled. "Wait a minute. Haven't I seen you somewhere before?"

"No, sir, I—I don't think so," Brad stammered.

The old man stepped out into the light. It was Jimmy! The man who had picked us up in the water taxi the night we were stranded in Bay Shore. What was he doing living in the haunted house?

"You're the kids who missed the ferry," Jimmy went on.

"Yes, sir," Brad replied cautiously.

"Well, you scared the livin' daylights out of me." His tone softened. "I was just about to go for a spin and maybe do a little clammin'. If you kids aren't doin' anything you can come along."

"Thanks. We'd love to," Kim answered quickly.

We crossed an open field to the bay side, where Jimmy's boat was docked. We all piled in and before we knew it Jimmy had zipped us over to the clam beds.

Jimmy told us that he was one of the few people who lived on Fire Island all year round. He kind of liked the life of a hermit and he kept to himself as much as possible. Most people didn't know he was Jimmy McGuire, the former sea captain. He made a living clamming and running his taxi service. He was such a character. He didn't even care if half the island thought he had been lost at sea thirty years ago. His fishing boat had been wrecked not too far from the coast in a bad storm. Fortunately for him, another boat had picked him up and brought him back to shore. He said all he wanted was privacy.

"Does everyone here know how to go clamming?" Ellen asked.

"There's nothing to it," Kim assured her. "Anybody can do it."

"It's a cinch," Brad added. "You just wade in the water and you can feel the little devils with the balls of your feet. It feels like you're stepping on a rock or something."

"Oh, gross," I groaned.

"It isn't gross at all." Kim laughed. "Then, after you've found the clam with your feet, you just bend down and dig it out with your hands. Simple."

"Clams don't bite or anything, do they?" Ellen wanted to know. I was wondering the same thing myself.

Jimmy turned around and burst out laughing. "Don't be ridiculous. They're harmless little critters."

El and I looked at each other skeptically.

"I'm game, I guess," El volunteered.

"Me too," I said, hesitating just a little.

Jimmy tossed the anchor overboard so the boat

wouldn't drift, and we all jumped out and waded into the shallow water.

"This here is the best spot along the whole Eastern Seaboard for clamming," Jimmy said.

He was right. In no time at all we had collected a couple of dozen. There was nothing to it. I didn't even realize it, but as we were clamming, Brad and I had wandered away from the group. This was the first time we'd been alone since the tournament the day before.

"Isn't this weird?" Brad commented.

"What?"

"That Jimmy's really old Captain McGuire."

"Yeah. I think it's neat."

We could see that Ellen and Kim were digging up a ton of clams.

"You must be glad to have Ellen here," Brad said. "She's really nice."

"She's my very best friend. I've missed her a whole lot this summer."

"I know what you mean. I get a little homesick for Kings Point every once in a while too. It's a drag."

I knew this was probably as good a time as any to tell him about Randy coming, but I wasn't sure I had the nerve.

"Is something wrong?" Brad asked.

"No. Why do you ask?"

"I don't know. You looked like you stepped on a crab or something."

"Well, I did want to tell you something."

"Shoot."

"Remember when I told you I had a boyfriend back home?"

"Yeah."

"Well, in a couple of weeks he's coming out here for a day."

"Oh, that's nice," he said tonelessly.

"You're not mad?"

"Why should I be mad? Hey, it's none of my business. I mean, I don't have a monopoly on you or anything."

"Well, I just wanted you to know. I guess I'll have to spend the whole day with him and I probably won't be able to see you."

"Sure. I understand. Don't worry. I'll stay out of the way."

Brad sure took it well. I didn't know why, but I really wanted him to be jealous. He didn't even seem to care. I thought he'd at least ask a few questions. If Catherine were coming to visit him, I'd probably have thrown a fit! Maybe Kim and Ellen were right about him. Just a little bit. Now that he'd gotten back at Jenny by beating her in the tournament, he had no use for me anymore. Or maybe this was just part of his act. Even if Brad was the slightest bit jealous, he'd never let on. We all knew he was much too cool to do anything like that.

We noticed that Ellen and Kim had just packed it in. Jimmy was loading their buckets of clams into the boat. Brad and I dug up a few more and then made our way back.

It had really been fun and I think Jimmy liked it too. He dropped Kim, Ellen, and me off at the dock in Ocean Bluffs, and then he went back to Sea Gate with Brad. By the time we got to A Summer Place, Ellen had less than an hour to pack up her stuff and catch the ferry home. I had to hastily get a note off to Randy so El could take it back with her. I wanted to let him know I was doing fine and tell him it was okay to visit.

It was kind of sad watching El get ready to leave. I hated to see her go. But, worst of all, I knew that the next time I'd see her I'd be back home in Garden City and the summer would be over. I might never see Brad again. But, after the way he had acted when I told him about Randy coming, maybe I didn't even care.

11

I glanced up at the kitchen calendar as I sipped my tea. Monday, August 30. I'd been both dreading it and looking forward to it at the same time. It was not just an ordinary day. Unfortunately it was the beginning of my last week on Fire Island. In no time at all I'd be back at school. The very thought of it was just too awful. After a whole summer of swimming and tennis and lying around in the sun, how could anybody expect me to get excited about algebra, chemistry, and Spanish? But I'd been looking forward to the day too. Randy was coming to visit. In fact, his ferry was due to arrive in ten minutes, and if I didn't get myself down to the dock pretty fast, I'd be in big trouble.

I put my teacup in the sink and then dashed to the bottom of the stairs. "See you later. I'm leaving to meet Randy," I shouted to no one in particular. I took off for the ferry like a shot.

I couldn't believe I hadn't seen Randy since June. It seemed like just a couple of days since he'd kissed me good-bye in front of my house. I knew it would be just like old times as soon as he stepped off the ferry. I couldn't wait to see him. I could really be myself with Randy. I guess that was the main difference between him and Brad. Sometimes when I was with Brad, I felt I was pretending to be someone I wasn't.

I had to admit one nice thing about Brad, though. He had promised to stay out of the way while Randy visited me. It wouldn't have been too cool if Randy and I went to Sprinkles or something and saw Brad. I could never have handled something like that. Knowing me, I'd probably just blurt everything out. "Hey, Randy, there's Brad Caldwell. We've been playing a lot of tennis together and we've been going out all summer, but it's really not a big deal, Randy. Oh, yeah, and if I can convince my parents, I'm going to visit Brad at college in the fall. You don't mind, do you?" Well, I'd never really say anything like that, but come to think of it, I wouldn't even have to. It would be written all over my face. Randy would know right off that something was going on.

The past few weeks with Brad had been a little strange. Sometimes I thought I really liked him and sometimes I wasn't so sure. I'd spent a lot of time thinking about the things Kim and Ellen said—that Brad was kind of conceited and would forget all about me when he went back to college. Mom hadn't said anything lately, but I just knew she wasn't really thrilled about him.

Long before the tournament even Elizabeth had

said she liked Randy better. Okay, so maybe they were right in some ways, I thought, but still, they had to see that Brad was gorgeous and a fantastic tennis player. Maybe he did think he was a little too cool and maybe he did have a girlfriend back home and maybe he did drink a little bit, but so what?

Leaving Brad wasn't going to be easy, no matter what everybody else thought about him. He'd never mentioned anything about my coming to Princeton again. Perhaps that was just as well. I didn't want to argue with my parents about it.

Oh, rats. From Bay Walk I could see that the ferry was already pulling in. I ran like crazy all the way to the dock. Luckily I got there just as Randy was getting off.

"Oh, Laur. It's great to see you."

He threw his arms around me and kissed me. I'd forgotten how nice it felt to be in his arms. It brought back some old memories. Like our very first kiss. It was in Randy's red Volkswagen. We were parked at a red light, talking about the football game we'd just been to. Then, right out of the blue, he moved over, put his arms around me, and kissed me. Just like that. It was great until the light changed and all the cars behind us started honking. But right then and there I knew Randy was something special. Well, I could tell one thing for sure. He hadn't lost his touch over the summer.

"You look gorgeous," he said.

"Thanks. You don't look so bad yourself. Great tan."

"I guess it's an occupational hazard." He laughed.

Randy really did look terrific. His long brown hair was streaked with red highlights from the sun and he had the most amazing tan I'd ever seen. I guess that's what Ellen meant when she said that being a lifeguard really agreed with him.

"Let's go back to the house so you can get settled," I suggested. "I'm dying to show you around."

As we walked back to A Summer Place, we weren't even paying any attention to the scenery. I guess it was because I hadn't seen Randy for so long. I just couldn't take my eyes off him for one minute. He was telling me all about working at the pool. Besides being a lifeguard, he also gave swimming lessons to little kids. I had to give him a lot of credit. I could never do anything like that. Could you imagine trying to keep a bunch of Elizabeths afloat? I'd go nuts.

"Did you ever save anybody?" I wanted to know.

"Well, sort of."

"Randy, how can you *sort of* save somebody? You either save them or you don't."

"Well, then I guess I did," he said.

"You're kidding! That's really fantastic! What happened?"

"I was on duty and some kid dove into some pretty shallow water and never came up. I pulled him out right away, gave him mouth to mouth, and he was fine. Just a little shaken up."

"Wow. You're a real hero. You saved the kid's life."

I could tell Randy was getting embarrassed.

"It was just a reflex. I guess it's just part of the job," he said.

I thought it was pretty great.

* * *

Schnapps practically jumped into Randy's arms as we walked through the kitchen and into the living room. Schnapps never forgets a friend. He wouldn't leave Randy alone.

"Boy, you're really lucky. It must have been a riot spending the whole summer here," Randy said, bending down to pat Schnapps on the head.

"I've been having a great time. All the kids are so much fun, and it's really nice to be able to go to the beach every day."

As I was talking, Randy wandered over to the fireplace and looked at the mantel. "Hey, what's this?" he asked.

"Uh—that's just a trophy," I stammered.

"I can see that. What did you do, enter a tournament or something?"

"Yeah. Just for fun."

"And you won it?"

"How about that?"

"Laur, that's fantastic. If you could do that, you'll make the tennis team for sure next year. You must have practiced like crazy."

"Yeah. I guess you could say I put a lot of time in."

"What made you go out for mixed doubles?"

"I don't know. I didn't really think I was good enough to compete in the singles competition."

"You should have told me."

"I wanted to surprise you."

That was the thing about Randy. He really trusted me. So why did I feel so crummy all of a sudden?

"It sure is a surprise. I think it's fantastic. I promise I'll go to all your matches next year. You'll probably be the star of the team."

"Assuming I get past tryouts, that is."

"You'll breeze right through. Hey, we're wasting good ray time. I want to see this famous Fire Island beach."

On the way down to the water we passed my parents walking hand in hand up Sandy Lane. We stopped to say hi for a minute. They were really glad to see Randy.

When we left them, Randy turned to me with a warm, knowing look. "See, Lauren, I told you everything would work out okay."

I didn't know why, but now that I was with Randy again I felt as if I didn't have a care in the world.

Because it was the last week of the season, the beach was crowded. Randy and I had to walk pretty far east before we could find a good spot to spread out our blanket.

We had just anchored it with our towels when I spotted Kim by the water.

"Hey," I said, "there's Kim. I told you about her. Come on, I'll introduce you."

We ran across the hot sand, trying not to step on other people's blankets.

"Kim. Over here," I called to her.

"Hi. I was looking all over for you."

"Kim, this is Randy."

"How ya doin'?" he said.

"Nice to meet you. Lauren talks about you all the time. So what are you guys up to today?"

"Not much. We'll probably hang out here most of the day. Randy's going back tonight."

"Well, you picked a good day to come, Randy. It's supposed to be a real scorcher. Nearly a hundred degrees. I guess that's why everybody's out here. I tried to make a sand castle before, but every time I started, it got trampled to death."

"I know what you mean," Randy sympathized. "I'm glad I'm not working today. The pool must be a madhouse."

Kim and I both saw them at the same time. Brad and Jenny. What were they doing here in Ocean Bluffs? They hardly ever came to our beach. And what were they doing *together?*

"I think I'm going to take a dip. Anyone want to join me?" Randy coaxed.

"No thanks," I declined. "It looks a little too rough out there for me right now. But you go ahead."

Kim stayed with me while Randy charged in, diving into the first big wave. He was a great swimmer.

"Did you see what I saw? What on earth is Caldwell doing here?" Kim asked.

"That's what I'd like to know."

"I'll bet anything they're spying on you."

"Oh, Kim, that's silly."

"Oh yeah? Then why are they suddenly so interested in Ocean Bluffs? And how come they've been within twenty feet of us ever since we got down here?"

"I can't believe them."

"Don't turn around. They're right behind you. Hey, by the way, Randy's really a doll."

"Thanks. I knew you'd like him."

We both watched him body surf. He rode a wave all the way into shore and then stood up and shook his hair out of his eyes. He looked so cute when he did that. As he ran toward us I admired his long, muscular torso.

"It's wicked out there," he said. "I really got thrown around a few times."

"I heard someone say the undertow's pretty bad today," Kim added.

"You girls better not go in until it calms down."

Kim made some excuse about having to go into Ocean Beach with her mother, but I knew she was only being polite. She probably figured Randy and I wanted to be alone. She was a real friend. Next to Ellen, I couldn't think of anyone I liked better. Except Randy and Brad, of course. And I wasn't even so sure about Brad right now. Was he really spying on me?

Randy and I spent the day talking, people watching, and walking up and down the beach. It was fun reminiscing about all the fun we'd had last year, Randy's swim meets, going out with El and Tom, sitting at our booth at the Fireplace.

I guess it was about half past three when we decided we just couldn't take the heat anymore. It must have been two hundred degrees in the shade. Randy checked out the water and it seemed to have calmed down quite a bit, so we thought we'd go for a swim.

We were having a terrific time playing in the waves. Randy was a lot braver than me, though. He rode them in, but I just dove under them and let them pass over me. I was watching Randy ride a huge wave into shore when all of a sudden I felt the most excruciating pain in my left leg. At first I thought I'd been stung by a jellyfish, but then I realized it was a cramp. My leg was as stiff as a board. I was doubled over in pain. The next thing I knew a monstrous wave slammed into me and pulled me under. I felt as though I'd been hit by a brick wall. Somehow I managed to lift my head out of the water, but there was no way I could even try to make it to shore. My leg was throbbing. It was in one big knot. I couldn't even move it. I had all I could do to stay afloat. I knew it would be all over if another wave plowed into me. My only hope was that Randy would see me. I waved my arms frantically to get his attention, but it was getting more and more difficult to keep my head up. I was tired and I kept swallowing water as I gasped for air. I wanted to yell for help, but I didn't even have the strength.

"Lauren, don't panic! It's going to be all right!"

Randy! I couldn't believe I'd really heard his voice. It seemed to be coming from my right. I tried swimming to him, but it was no use.

"Just stay calm!" As he shouted to me I could see him swimming toward me out of the corner of my eye.

"Try to relax and let me bring you in."

He gently grabbed my left wrist and turned me around. Then he secured one arm around me and pulled me along as he swam sidestroke. When the water got too shallow to swim, he picked me up and carried me safely to shore. I lay down on the sand and then he carefully massaged my calf muscle. I could feel the tension slowly releasing. One of the Ocean Beach guards came right over and wrapped a blanket around me. I couldn't stop sobbing.

"Just relax and take some deep breaths," Randy said soothingly.

Once I caught my breath I began to feel a little better, but I was pretty shaken up. My eyes burned and I felt nauseous from swallowing so much salt-water, but it was so good to be on land again I didn't even care.

A crowd had begun to gather around us. As Randy held me in his arms, rocking me back and forth, I noticed Brad standing off to the side.

After a few minutes Randy helped me up and then carefully supported me as I hobbled back to the house. I was glad no one was home. I just wasn't up to answering a million questions. And Mom would have absolutely flipped out if she'd seen me limping up the walk. I lay down on the living room sofa so Randy could prop up my leg on a pillow. Then he brought me a glass of lemonade.

"Here, drink this," he said. "It'll make you feel better."

I closed my eyes for a second, and the next thing I knew Randy was standing over me trying to wake me up for dinner. I was so mad at myself. He was leaving in a little over an hour and I had spent half the afternoon sleeping.

"Why didn't you wake me?" I asked, rubbing my eyes.

"I thought the rest would do you good."

"But I wanted to talk to you."

"Don't worry. Elizabeth kept me company. We played Scrabble."

"Oh, you poor kid. Maybe *you* should lie down and rest," I joked.

A horrible thought crossed my mind. What if the little genius had said something about Brad? If she did, boy, she'd really be in for it! Even Elizabeth should have had more sense than to do something as dumb as that. I knocked on wood, just to be sure.

After dinner Randy didn't want me to walk down to the ferry with him, but I insisted. I felt a whole lot better, and besides, I wanted to be with him as long as possible. We sat on the edge of the dock, dangling our feet over the water. I knew I'd be back home in another week or so, but still, it was sad to see him go.

"I've been meaning to ask you something all day, Laur, but I just never got around to it."

"What's that?"

"Well, the pool is having a big end-of-the-year barbecue this Saturday night, and I was hoping you'd be able to come. It's kind of the last big bash for all the guards, you know?"

"I'd love to come, Randy, but there's only one little problem. I don't know if we'll be back in Garden City by Saturday. I'm not sure, but I think we may be staying out here until Sunday."

"Oh, I hope not. It just wouldn't be any fun without you."

"I don't know what to say, Randy. I'll have to find out from Mom when we're going home and I'll let you know."

"Call me up as soon as you find out."

"I promise. I'll call you first thing."

The ferry was on its way in. It had stopped in Ocean Beach first, so there were lots of passengers on board already.

"Randy, I don't really know how to say this but,

well, I just don't know how to thank you for saving me. I hate to think what would have happened if . . ."

"Oh, come on, Lauren. It wasn't anything. Anybody else would have done the same thing."

"Well, I think you're really terrific."

I kissed him tenderly on the lips, and then he held me close and kissed me again. I didn't want him to leave.

"All aboard for Bay Shore," the first mate yelled.

"I guess this is it. I sure hope you'll be able to come to the barbecue, Laur," Randy said, reaching into his pocket for his ferry ticket.

"Me too. I'll call you in a couple of days."

He walked over the plank and onto the ferry, and in a minute or two I could see him waving to me from the deck. I lingered on the dock watching the boat sail away until it was so small I couldn't see it anymore. I felt kind of weird. Like I might laugh and cry at the same time. I was happy because we had spent such a wonderful day together, but I was sad, too, because I missed him like crazy already.

I unfastened the heart-shaped locket that was hanging around my neck and opened it up. I don't know why, but I hardly ever opened it. In fact, half the time I forgot I was wearing it. The little pictures of the two of us were still in pretty good shape. I remember when Elizabeth took them with Dad's Polaroid. Randy and I had to pose a few times, standing farther and farther away from her, until our heads came out small enough. I held the locket in my hand all the way home and kept looking at Randy's photo. It would just have to do until I could see him again.

The phone was ringing when I walked into the house. Could be Kim, I thought. She was probably wondering how the day went. Wait until she hears I almost drowned.

"Lauren, is that you?" Mom shouted as I came in.

"Yeah."

"Telephone."

"Thanks," I said, picking up in the living room. "Hello."

"Hi. I've been worried about you."

"Brad!" I was surprised to hear his voice.

"I'm glad you're home. How are you?"

"I'm okay. By the way, I saw you and Jenny on the beach today."

"Yeah. It was so hot you couldn't even find a spot on the beach in Sea Gate, so we thought we'd go down to the Bluffs and check it out. Are you sure you're okay?"

"Positive. I was just a little shaken up, that's all."

"You're pretty lucky to have a lifeguard for a boyfriend."

"I suppose I am."

"So listen, I'm calling to ask you something really special."

"What's that, Brad?"

"At the end of the season the club has a posh dinner party with dancing and everything. Everyone gets all dressed up. It's really elegant. Kind of the last big evening of the summer. I know you'd love it, Lauren. Want to go?"

Randy had left only fifteen minutes before, and Brad was already asking me out. This whole mess is going to drive me nuts, I thought. I couldn't even think straight. I twisted my locket nervously around my fingers, searching for an answer.

"When is it?"

"Saturday night."

Oh, brother. That figured. "I don't even know if we're going to be here then, Brad. My parents haven't decided whether we're going home on Saturday or Sunday." I sounded like a broken record.

"Oh, it would be a real bummer if you left Saturday. Everybody stays till Sunday. You can talk them into it, can't you?"

"I don't know. Can I tell you in a couple of days?" I stalled.

"Yeah, sure. But believe me, you wouldn't want to miss this party. It's the best."

"I'll see what I can do."

"Sweet dreams and stay out of trouble."

I poured myself a glass of iced tea and sat down at the kitchen table. Another typical Lauren McDermott disaster, I thought. I suppose everything depends on when we go home. If we leave Saturday I'll be in great shape. Then I'll be back in Garden City and I'll be able to go to the barbecue with Randy. But if we leave on Sunday I'm really stuck. I won't be able to go to the barbecue with Randy, and I'll have no excuse to give Brad. I'll have to go to the end-of-the-season party at the club. It seemed like there was no way out. I hoped Mom and Dad would hurry up and decide when we were going home. For all I cared, we could leave anytime, I thought. I'd had enough of summer. I just wanted to be back in Garden City. Seeing Randy had really made me homesick.

* * *

"Well, you've had quite a day, haven't you, Lauren?" Mom said, placing some coffee mugs in the sink.

"It was great to see Randy again."

"He's quite a young man."

"Yeah, I guess. Hey, Mom, when are we going home?" I asked eagerly.

"Are you that anxious?"

"No, I was just wondering. I want to make some plans."

"Probably Sunday."

I must have looked like the world had just come to an end. That meant I couldn't go to Randy's barbecue and I couldn't say no to Brad. The worst possible situation.

"Why the glum expression, dear?"

"It's kind of a long story. Randy invited me to a barbecue in Garden City on Saturday night and I really want to go. If we're leaving Sunday I guess I can't. The other problem is that Brad invited me to a party on the same night. I don't want to go, but I don't know how to tell him. I was kind of hoping we'd be leaving Saturday. That would solve everything."

"Oh, I see. That is rather complicated. We've already made all the arrangements to go back Sunday, Lauren, so I don't think we could change anything." Mom paused for a minute, wrinkling her brow. "But, you know, there might be a way," she continued. "If you really want to go to Randy's barbecue, why don't you take the ferry over on Saturday? He could meet you and take you to the barbecue and then you could spend Saturday night at Ellen's house. I'm sure that would be all right. And we'd be home by Sunday afternoon."

"Oh, Mom, that would be fantastic! Thanks a million!"

I ran up to my room and closed the door. I didn't feel like talking to anyone—well, maybe Ellen, but she was all the way across the bay. I'd call her the next day and make sure I could stay overnight on Saturday. Then I'd call Randy and tell him the good news!

Only one problem. How could I tell Brad I couldn't go to the party? I could tell him that my whole family was leaving on Saturday, but that wouldn't be right. With my luck he'd run into Elizabeth on Sunday morning and then he'd know I'd lied to him. I would have hated to have something like that happen.

It was strange, but I didn't feel quite the same way about Brad. I guess it had all started the night we went to Bay Shore, but I had pushed it back. He had wanted me to go to a bar with him, and then he had read the schedule wrong and made us late. And he hadn't even stayed to help me explain the whole mess to my parents! And he had never told me anything about Catherine, even when I had told him about Randy. The real clincher was when he had turned up at Ocean Bluffs with Jenny. Everybody knows that Ocean Bluffs is twice as packed as Sea Gate on a hot day . . . I knew he just wanted to check Randy out.

I began to wonder if it had all been worth it. True, Brad was gorgeous, we'd had lots of fun together, and if I made the tennis team it would be all because of his coaching; but on the other hand, I had a pretty special guy at home. Maybe Ellen had been right. Brad did seem sort of immature at times. And he was pretty conceited. Still, I didn't want to hurt him. I would just have to find a way to tell him that I couldn't go to the party at the club with him.

12

A Summer Place was a complete shambles. Packing is definitely the pits. I wanted to help but I didn't know where to begin. I couldn't even walk across the living room floor. It was wall-to-wall boxes. The whole scene had Schnapps totally confused. All he wanted to do was stay out of the way, but he couldn't even find his bed. We had invaded his territory and turned it inside out. As far as I was concerned, packing up down here was the easy part. I hadn't even attempted to get my stuff together yet. I sure had accumulated enough of it. I just couldn't bring myself to throw anything out. Like the special sea shells I'd collected. Or the ashtray from the club. I still had a book of matches from Sprinkles, my ticket stub from *Rebel in Disguise*, the players' schedules from the tournament, a clam shell from Jimmy, a menu from Barnacle Bill's. Get the picture? My assortment of memorabilia was endless. By the time I got finished with all the souvenirs, there might not be room for my clothes and tennis gear. Oh, and then there was my trophy, of course. Mom had promised to carry that with her personally. If I hadn't been leaving a day early to go to Randy's barbecue, I'd have taken care of it myself.

"Lauren, why don't you go upstairs and start packing your things?" Mom suggested. "I'll finish up here."

"I don't think I can find the stairs."

"Very funny. Just follow the path through the middle of the room."

When I got upstairs, the whole room smelled like my favorite scent. Elizabeth must have been hitting the perfume bottle again. She was rushing around more frantically than ever, and she definitely looked as though she was up to something.

"Elizabeth, do you have any idea why it smells like a perfume factory in here?"

"Uh, would you believe it smelled funny in here, so I sprayed some around the room?"

"Nice try, but no. Just ask me first next time, okay?"

"Sure."

"Elizabeth," Mom called, "Billy Caldwell's here to see you."

"Billy's here to see you?" I teased. "Very interesting."

"I've got to go now. Bye," she muttered. She checked her hair in the mirror and dashed downstairs.

For someone who always swore she'd never like

boys, good old Elizabeth sure was changing fast. Next thing you know, she'd be borrowing my make-up too. I laughed to myself and started transferring things from my cramped dresser drawers into the big blue suitcase on my bed.

I was kind of glad I was leaving before it got too crazy around here. Everything had worked out just great. Ellen's mom said I could stay overnight, so that wasn't a problem, and Randy was going to meet my ferry in Bay Shore later that afternoon. Seeing him last week had been fantastic, but it had made me miss him more than ever. I'd really been looking forward to the barbecue. In fact, I'd thought of little else all week.

It took me a couple of days to get up enough nerve to tell Brad I couldn't go to the party at the club. We were eating ice cream cones at Sprinkles and I had sort of sprung it on him. I couldn't think of a good excuse so I just spilled out the truth. Really, though, when I thought about it, going to the barbecue with Randy was the only fair thing I could do. I mean, he did ask me first. But you know something? Even if Brad had asked me first, I think I still would have gone with Randy. Brad didn't even flinch when I told him the news. After all, who was I kidding? A guy like him probably knew at least ten other girls who'd be dying to go to the party with him. If he was disappointed he sure disguised it pretty well. "That's cool," he said. "But you're going to miss one wicked party." Naturally Brad and I are still good friends. I didn't want to totally break things off. In a lot of ways, I guess I'll always kind of like him just a little. As a matter of fact, he was coming to say good-bye. I hate stuff like that.

I never thought I'd do it, but I finally finished packing. Why does it always seem like you have so much more stuff when it's time to go home? I was sure my things had multiplied in the drawers. Actually it wasn't all that bad. Only one suitcase and a couple of boxes. Well, maybe a few boxes. Five or so, really, but that was okay. After all, it was a whole summer's worth of junk. After I took inventory for about the third time, I was satisfied that I hadn't forgotten anything important. I closed my suitcase and wandered downstairs to see how everything was going with the crew down below.

Great timing on my part. They were just about finished when I offered to help. I was really glad they didn't need me. You know how it is. I wanted to have my last couple of hours on Fire Island all to myself.

I went outside and sat down on the deck. It was kind of a grayish day. Maybe the sky was doing that on purpose so I wouldn't feel so bad about leaving. I hated the thought of saying good-bye to A Summer Place. I'd never lived anywhere so special in my whole life. Sometimes it seemed that the house had a personality all its own. I knew I'd miss it terribly. I heard the familiar sound of the back door squeaking. I prayed it wasn't Elizabeth coming outside to bug me.

"A pretty good summer, wouldn't you say, Lauren?" Dad pulled up a chair and sat down beside me.

"It was the best summer I've ever had." Like a flash I thought about last summer when Dad was living in the city. I felt so lonely all the time. I just hung out at the Garden City pool a lot and spent hours in my room listening to records and talking to Ellen.

"I think this was just what we needed, don't you?" Dad asked.

"What do you mean?"

"You know—to bring everyone together again, the way it used to be."

I couldn't believe this was coming from Dad. He hardly ever spoke to me so openly. I didn't really know what to say. "I'm sure glad things are back to normal, but sometimes it's still a little scary," I confessed.

"Scary?"

"Well, I know this sounds really dumb, but I worry sometimes that you and Mom might separate again."

"Honey, you, Elizabeth, and your mother mean everything in the world to me. I'd never do anything to hurt you. Mom and I had our problems, but they're all behind us now. I promise you." He put his arms around me and hugged me really tight. I felt like I was a little kid again. Dad used to pick me up and carry me piggy-back style or let me sit on his lap while we watched TV. "Remember how I used to take you out on Saturday mornings?" Dad went on, sounding pretty sentimental.

"Sure. I loved it. We'd go horseback riding or shopping or swimming."

"One thing I've realized this summer, Lauren, is that I rarely spend any time with you and Elizabeth anymore. We'll have to do something about that this fall, don't you agree?"

"I couldn't think of anything nicer."

He looked at his watch and sighed. "Well, I promised your mother I'd go down to the ferry slip before noon and finalize the arrangements for our departure." He started to grin and shake his head. "Would you believe that Schnapps needs a special pass to take the ferry? They only allow four dogs on each boat."

"Is that first class or coach?" I giggled.

"Knowing old Schnapps, he'll probably insist on first class." He smiled and touched his hand to my cheek as he got up to go inside. I couldn't imagine what made him talk to me so candidly, but I didn't care. I guess things really were going to be like they used to be.

I knew Brad would be coming over any minute, so I walked around to the front of the house. As soon as I turned toward the street I saw him coming down Sandy Lane. I met him halfway between my house and the beach.

"All packed?" he asked.

"Yeah. How about you?"

"Nah. We're not heading out till Monday. I leave all the packing till the last minute. It gets me depressed. I hate to see summer end."

"Me too. But in a way I'll be glad to get home. Aren't you looking forward to going to college?"

"Oh, sure. I can't wait to play soccer and tennis in the Ivy League, but still, there's nothing like playing tennis at the club and catching rays every day. If you ask me, it's pure heaven out here."

We walked down to the beach and sat down on the sand. It was a little bit overcast, so there weren't that many people out. We did have some company, though. A couple of sea gulls waddled over to us and another one came in for a landing right over our heads. When a breaker rolled in, they ran like crazy so they wouldn't get wet. I thought they were adorable. They could really move too.

"These gulls really have it made. They can come and go as they please and do whatever they want." Brad sighed.

"Yeah, but they can't play tennis," I joked.

"Good point. I guess we're one up on 'em. Do you think you'll be coming back here next year?"

"I haven't a clue. Nobody's said a word."

"Just think. We could sweep the mixed doubles title again. Two years in a row. Wouldn't that be great?"

"Sure would. But if Jenny learns to hit a backhand, we might run into some trouble."

"Don't worry. She's beyond hope. You, on the other hand, are going to be a real ace by next year. And I know you're going to knock 'em dead on that school tennis team of yours."

"That's if I make it."

"I'd bet my racket on it."

"I guess I had a good coach. I think you may know him."

"Yeah. You might say we're real close. We kind of look alike too," he said, grinning.

I fell into Brad's arms laughing. As we gently toppled over into the sand, he pressed his lips firmly against mine. It was as if we both knew it was our last kiss ever. Kind of like telling each other it had been a great summer and we'd had lots of fun, but now it was all over. Time for us to go our separate ways. We lingered in each other's arms for a long time, listening to the shrill cries of the gulls overhead and the quiet lull of the waves rolling into shore.

"Well, I'm not very good at this good-bye stuff," Brad whispered, brushing the sand from my hair, "so keep in touch, okay?"

"Okay."

"I'll send you my address in Princeton. Maybe you'll come see me sometime."

"Maybe." Deep down inside I knew I wouldn't.

He leaned over and quickly kissed me again.

"I'll be seein' ya, Lauren. Have a good trip home."

"Bye, Brad. Good luck in college."

I watched him walk slowly along the water back to Sea Gate. Every so often he'd pick up a sea shell and toss it into the ocean. When he was about a hundred feet or so down the beach, he suddenly stopped, turned around, and waved to me in one smooth motion. I hoped he couldn't see the tears in my eyes.

I must have scared the daylights out of the poor gulls when I got up to walk down to the water. They flew off in a million different directions. It was getting pretty cloudy and I didn't feel like hanging out at the beach all alone, so I headed over to Kim's. She probably wanted to take a break from packing.

I knocked on her front door but nobody answered. I figured she was probably out back, so I walked around to the patio.

"Anybody home?" I shouted.

"Back here," Kim answered. She was standing behind the outdoor shower, hanging clothes on the line. "We're just about all set," she went on. "How about you?"

"I'm all ready too. It's kind of sad, in a way, to be leaving and all, but I guess it'll be nice to get home." I handed her a bunch of clothespins from a basket on the ground.

"That's what Lydia always says. The best part about going on vacation is coming home. I'll tell you a secret, though. Sometimes I wish we were going back to Boston instead of moving to Port Washington. You'll have to come up with me sometime when I visit Dad. You'd love it there." She finished hanging the clothes and we collapsed into a couple of chaise longues on the patio.

"I'd love to, but I'll bet you're going to like Long Island just as much once I show you around."

"You're probably right. I guess I should at least give it a chance."

"For sure. Hey, guess what? I just said good-bye to Brad."

"How'd it go?"

"Like I expected. We said we really had a great summer together and he said he'd keep in touch. He mentioned visiting him in Princeton again too."

"What did you say to that?"

"Not much. I just sort of hedged. I don't know, but I just have this funny feeling that I'll never see him again."

"You didn't do anything dumb like cry, did you?"

"No. I was fine."

"Good. That's probably how it'll be with me and Mike too. I really don't expect to see him much once he's away at school. But who knows? Maybe we'll come back here next summer and we'll all be together again. Wouldn't that be great?"

"Yeah. I guess it would be fun. Listen, I've got to

get back. I'm leaving in a couple of hours and I still have to wash my hair."

"Have a good time."

"Are you kidding? I can't wait to see Randy again. I've been counting the minutes."

"I'll call you at home next week. We should be all moved in by then."

"Sounds great, Kim. See you back home."

"Say hi to Randy for me."

When I got home, all I really had to do was take a shower and get fixed up for the barbecue that night. Everything else was done. I'll say one thing. As I slipped into my jeans and my white cotton peasant shirt, I sure was glad I wasn't putting on some frilly old dress to go to a fancy party at the club! For a little color, I added a pair of red enamel earrings, red espadrilles, and a tiny red canvas shoulder bag. I glanced in the mirror and fluffed up my hair. Thank goodness Elizabeth had left me some perfume. It was Randy's favorite.

I threw my overnight stuff into my tennis bag and went downstairs. You'd think I was going to China or something the way everyone fussed and carried on and kissed me good-bye. Even Schnapps. He jumped up on his hind legs and yapped hysterically. He didn't shut up until I picked him up and cradled him in my arms. He's the only dog in the world who thinks he's a baby. The whole scene was getting a little dramatic. I'd only be gone overnight. That is, if they ever let me out.

I don't know how I did it, but I finally escaped. It wasn't easy. Have you ever been happy and sad at the same time? Well, that's exactly how I felt when I waved to everyone. It was great to see them all together, and after talking to Dad that morning, it seemed that things just couldn't be better.

On my way to the ferry I quietly said good-bye to all my favorite places. A Summer Place, Sandy Lane, Bay Walk, Sprinkles, Kim's house, the tennis courts where Brad and I first played . . . If we came back next year it would be great to see them again. And if we didn't, I knew I'd always remember them fondly.

As soon as the ferry pulled in I got on and climbed upstairs. When I thought about it, I realized I hadn't crossed the bay since the night Brad and I had gone into Bay Shore. What a fiasco that had been! It sure wasn't funny at the time, but I laughed to myself as I remembered it. Poor Brad. He must have felt like a first-class nerd. Well, he should have, anyway. He sure acted like one. I think that night it finally began to dawn on me. You know, that Brad wasn't the big hero I thought he was. Still, we'd had our good times together and I knew I'd never forget him.

My mind kept wandering the whole trip. It didn't seem possible that we could have crossed the bay already, but I saw the first mate leave the captain's cabin to go down below. A sure sign that we were getting close to shore. When we finally docked, I was actually happy to set foot on Long Island.

A crowd of people had gathered on the dock to meet the ferry. I was looking everywhere for Randy. He spotted me first.

"Hey, Lauren!" I heard him call.

I made my way through the crowd as fast as I could. "It's great to be home," I sighed.

"It's great to have you back."

We hugged and kissed as though we hadn't seen

each other in a hundred years. I couldn't even begin to describe how nice it felt to be together again.

"Come on. My car's in the lot," he said, leading the way.

It had been more than three months since I'd sat in the Beetle, but as soon as I got in and slammed the wobbly door, it seemed as though it had been only yesterday. I glanced over to the driver's seat and watched Randy carefully maneuver the bug out of the jammed parking lot. It was like old times. Just the two of us, doing the things we loved to do. Maybe Brad *was* tall and blond and a big tennis star, and maybe he *was* going to college, but Randy was in a class by himself. To me, he was worth a million Brads.

There seemed to be a steady stream of passengers still coming off the ferry. They were getting into cars, boarding buses, waiting for rides, making telephone calls. I wondered if they'd had as much fun as I did on Fire Island. I wondered, too, if they were as happy as I was to be home.

If I go back to Fire Island next summer, could it possibly be as good as it was last summer? I knew one thing for sure. That summer was something pretty special. It was a summer I'd remember for a long, long time, a summer full of memories and friends I'd cherish forever.

Three exciting First Love from Silhouette romances yours for 15 days—_free!_

If you enjoyed this First Love from Silhouette® you'll want to read more! These are true-to-life romances about the things that matter most to you now—your friendships, dating, getting along in school, and learning about yourself. The stories could really happen, and the characters are so real they'll seem like friends.

Now you can get 3 First Love from Silhouette romances to look over for 15 days—absolutely free! If you decide not to keep them, simply return them and pay nothing. But if you enjoy them as much as we believe you will, keep them and pay the invoice enclosed with your trial shipment. You'll then become a member of the First Love from Silhouette℠ Book Club and will receive 3 more new First Love from Silhouette romances every month. You'll always be among the first to get them, and you'll never miss a new title. There is no minimum number of books to buy and you can cancel at any time. To receive your 3 books, mail the coupon below today.

First Love from Silhouette® is a service mark and a registered trademark of Simon & Schuster.

This offer expires December 31, 1983

 **First Love from Silhouette Book Club, Dept. FL-015
120 Brighton Road, P.O. Box 5020, Clifton, NJ 07012**

Please send me 3 First Love from Silhouette romances to keep for 15 days, absolutely _free_. I understand I am not obligated to join the First Love from Silhouette Book Club unless I decide to keep them.

NAME_____
(Please print)

ADDRESS_____

CITY_____ STATE_____ ZIP_____

Signature_____
(If under 18, parent or guardian must sign)

First Love from Silhouette

38 ☐ ALL-AMERICAN GIRL
Payton

39 ☐ BE MY VALENTINE
Harper

40 ☐ MY LUCKY STAR
Cassiday

41 ☐ JUST FRIENDS
Francis

42 ☐ PROMISES TO COME
Dellin

43 ☐ A KNIGHT TO REMEMBER
Martin

44 ☐ SOMEONE LIKE
JEREMY VAUGHN
Alexander

45 ☐ A TOUCH OF LOVE
Madison

46 ☐ SEALED WITH A KISS
Davis

47 ☐ THREE WEEKS OF LOVE
Aks

48 ☐ SUMMER ILLUSION
Manning

49 ☐ ONE OF A KIND
Brett

50 ☐ STAY, SWEET LOVE
Fisher

51 ☐ PRAIRIE GIRL
Coy

52 ☐ A SUMMER TO REMEMBER
Robertson

FOR AN ILLUMINATING EXPERIENCE
THIS JULY READ
LIGHT OF MY LIFE
BY ELAINE HARPER.

FIRST LOVE, Department FL/4
1230 Avenue of the Americas
New York, NY 10020

Please send me the books I have checked above. I am enclos-
ing $_____ (please add 50¢ to cover postage and handling.
NYS and NYC residents please add appropriate sales tax).
Send check or money order—no cash or C.O.D.'s please.
Allow six weeks for delivery.

NAME _____

ADDRESS _____

CITY_____ STATE/ZIP_____

First Love from Silhouette

Coming Next Month

Light Of My Life by Elaine Harper

Lucille discovers that her job behind the scenes has more drama than life on stage—especially after her electrifying encounter with David. It is a delightfully enlightening experience.

Picture Perfect by Carrie Enfield

Almost everyone wished that pesky Liane with her embarrassingly candid shots would blow away. Only Alan appreciated her gift for catching the right moment. He encouraged her to perfect her technique.

Love On The Run by Leslie Graham

Kate was only a sophomore in high school, but she had fallen in love with Brian, the charismatic senior class president. Did she stand a chance or was she only a fellow runner to him?

Romance In Store by Elaine Arthur

Carol had a flair for business, the manager of the fashion department had told her so. But did she also have a flair for romance? Should she discard her last year's model now that the season had changed?